Dear parents, caregivers, and educators:

If you want to get your child excited about reading, you've come to the right place! Ready-to-Read *GRAPHICS* is the perfect launchpad for emerging graphic novel readers.

All Ready-to-Read *GRAPHICS* books include the following:

- ★ **A how-to guide to reading graphic novels for first-time readers**

- ★ **Easy-to-follow panels to support reading comprehension**

- ★ **Accessible vocabulary to build your child's reading confidence**

- ★ **Compelling stories that star your child's favorite characters**

- ★ **Fresh, engaging illustrations that provide context and promote visual literacy**

Wherever your child may be on their reading journey, Ready-to-Read *GRAPHICS* will make them giggle, gasp, and want to keep reading more.

Blast off on this starry adventure . . . a universe of graphic novel reading awaits!

Geraldine Pu

and Her Cat Hat, Too!

Written and illustrated by Maggie P. Chang

Ready-to-Read *GRAPHICS*

Simon Spotlight

New York   London   Toronto   Sydney   New Delhi

For my brother

SIMON SPOTLIGHT
An imprint of Simon & Schuster Children's Publishing Division
1230 Avenue of the Americas, New York, New York 10020
This Simon Spotlight edition January 2022
Copyright © 2022 by Margaret Chang
SIMON SPOTLIGHT, READY-TO-READ, and colophon are registered
trademarks of Simon & Schuster, Inc.
For information about special discounts for bulk purchases, please contact
Simon & Schuster Special Sales at 1-866-506-1949 or business@simonandschuster.com.
Manufactured in the United States of America 1221 LAK
2 4 6 8 10 9 7 5 3 1
Library of Congress Cataloging-in-Publication Data
Names: Chang, Maggie P., author, illustrator.
Title: Geraldine Pu and her cat hat, too! / written and illustrated by Maggie P. Chang.
Description: Simon Spotlight edition. | New York : Simon Spotlight, 2022.
Series: Geraldine Pu | Summary: Geraldine Pu thinks her hair is boring and uses her cat
shaped hat to cover it, but after she tries to copy her grandmother's hair with disastrous
results, Geraldine learns to embrace her individuality.
Identifiers: LCCN 2021034225 (print) | LCCN 2021034226 (ebook)
ISBN 9781534484719 (paperback) | ISBN 9781534484726 (hardcover)
ISBN 9781534484733 (ebook)
Subjects: CYAC: Graphic novels. | Hats—Fiction. | Individuality—Fiction.
Self-acceptance—Fiction. | Hair—Fiction. | Taiwanese Americans—Fiction.
LCGFT: Graphic novels.
Classification: LCC PZ7.7.C419 Gd 2021 (print) | LCC PZ7.7.C419 (ebook) |
DDC 741.5/973—dc23
LC record available at https://lccn.loc.gov/2021034225
LC ebook record available at https://lccn.loc.gov/2021034226

Contents

How to Read This Book

This is Geraldine. She's here to give you some tips on reading this book.

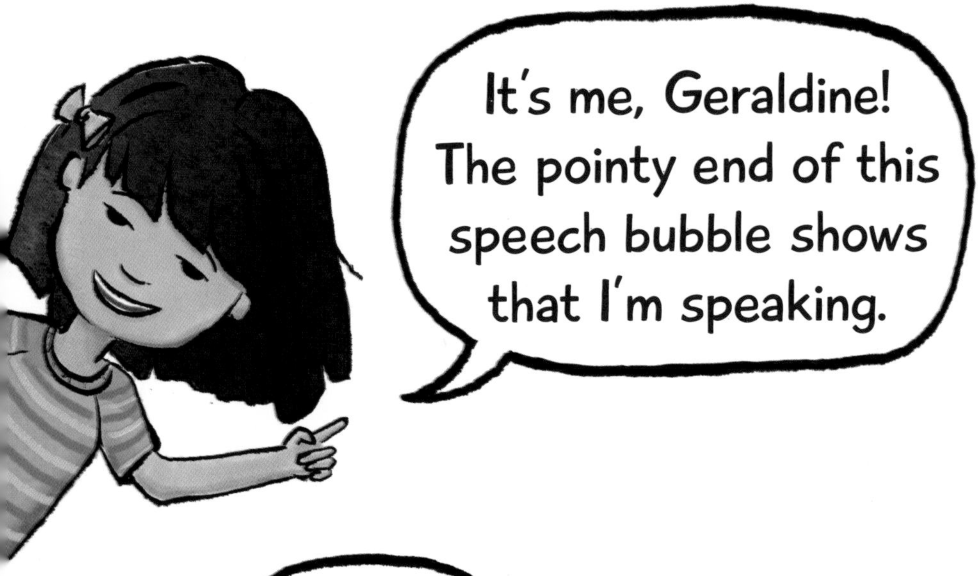
It's me, Geraldine! The pointy end of this speech bubble shows that I'm speaking.

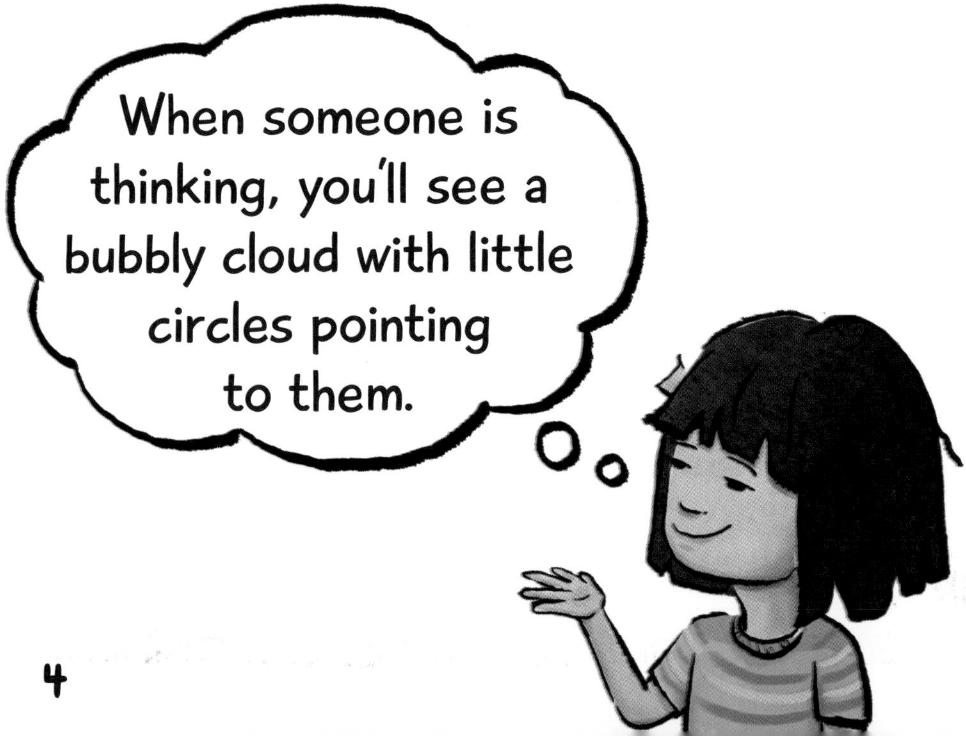
When someone is thinking, you'll see a bubbly cloud with little circles pointing to them.

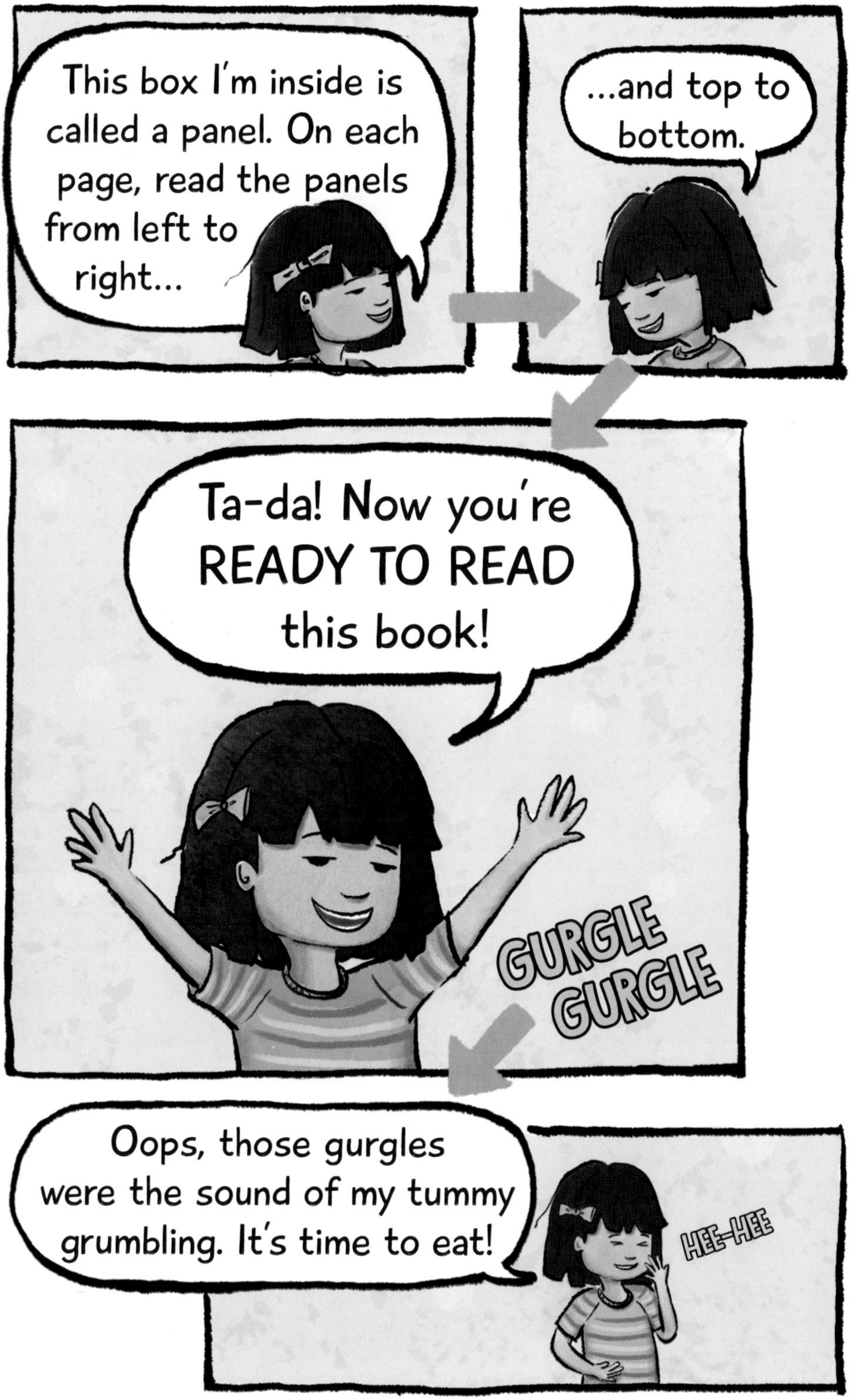
This box I'm inside is called a panel. On each page, read the panels from left to right...
...and top to bottom.
Ta-da! Now you're READY TO READ this book!
GURGLE GURGLE
Oops, those gurgles were the sound of my tummy grumbling. It's time to eat!
HEE-HEE

Words from Geraldine's World

Geraldine and her family speak English, Mandarin Chinese, and Taiwanese. Mandarin Chinese and Taiwanese are both languages spoken in Taiwan. Some of Geraldine's family members used to live there!

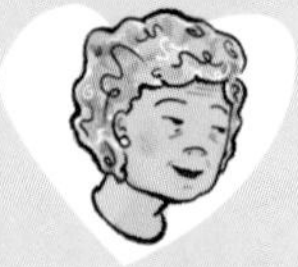

Amah (said like this: ah-MAH): the word for "Grandma" in Taiwanese.

mao (said like this: MOW, rhymes with "wow"): the word for "cat" in Mandarin Chinese.

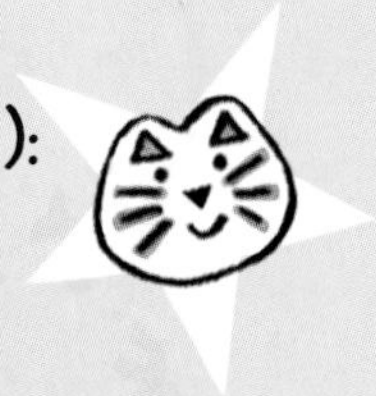

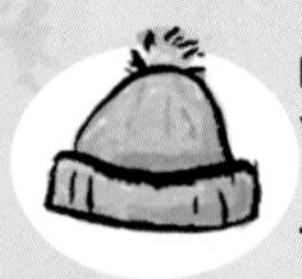

maotz (said like this: MOW-tzz): the word for "hat" in Mandarin Chinese. Put "mao" and "maotz" together, and you get "cat hat."

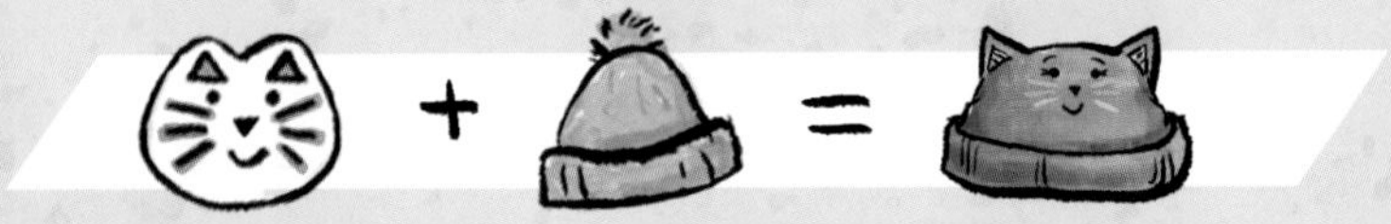

A note on the spellings in this book:
There are different ways to write Mandarin Chinese and Taiwanese words in the English alphabet, but our book spells them the way Geraldine likes to spell them.

Chapter One

Meet Geraldine Pu. Her last name rhymes with "two" and "moo."

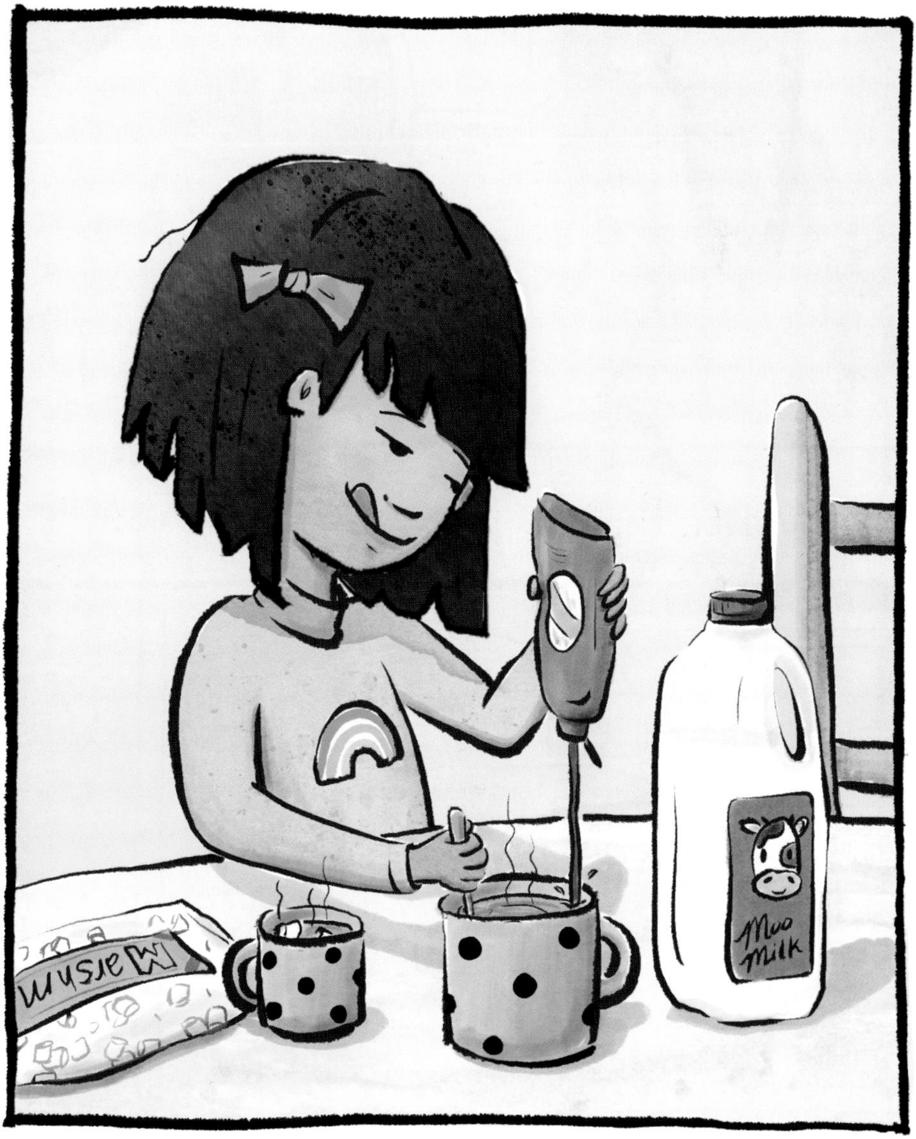
Moo Milk

Geraldine loves her family,

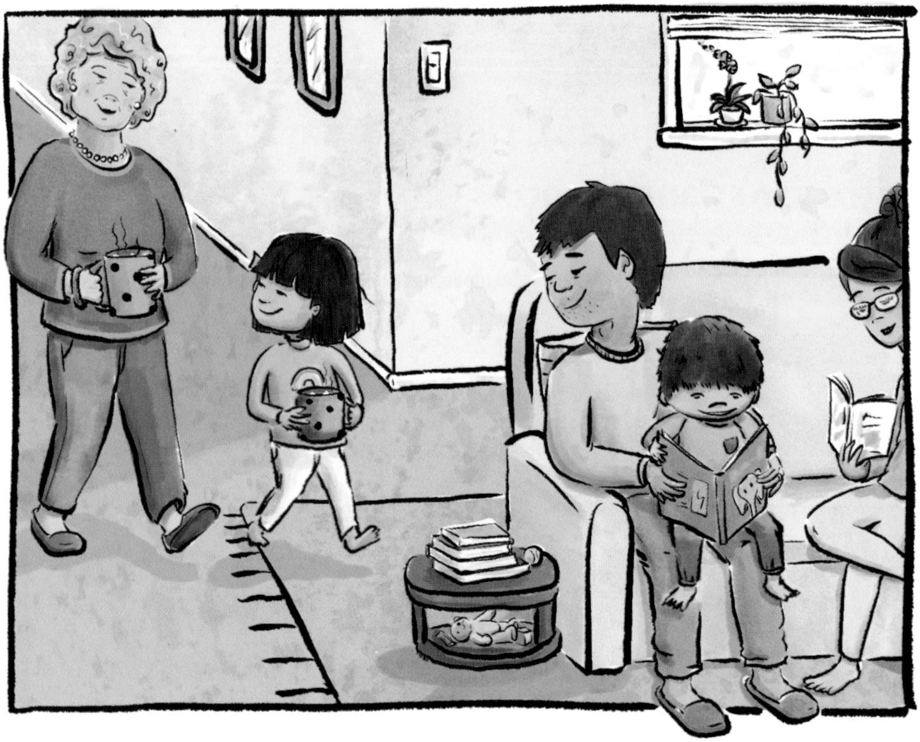

her favorite things,

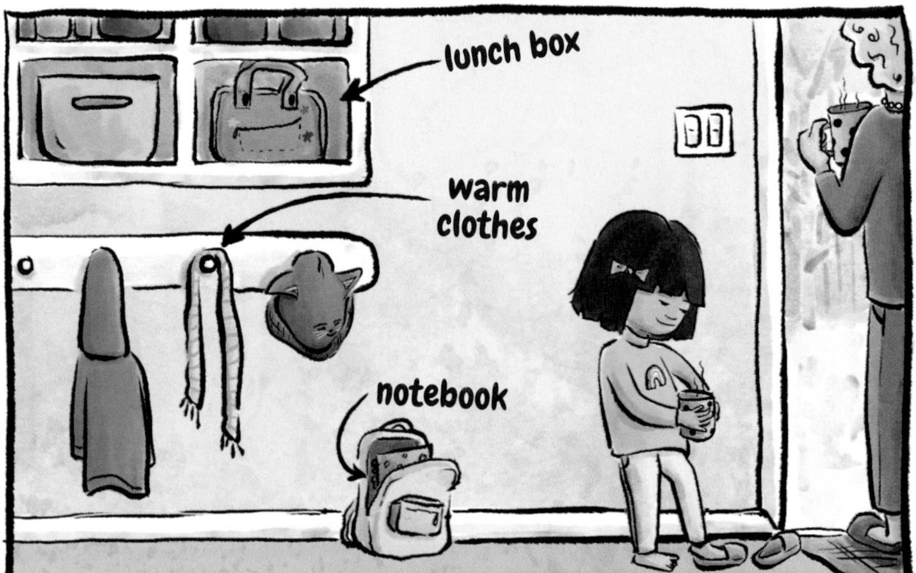
lunch box
warm clothes
notebook

and chilly weather. She adores getting comfy and cozy.

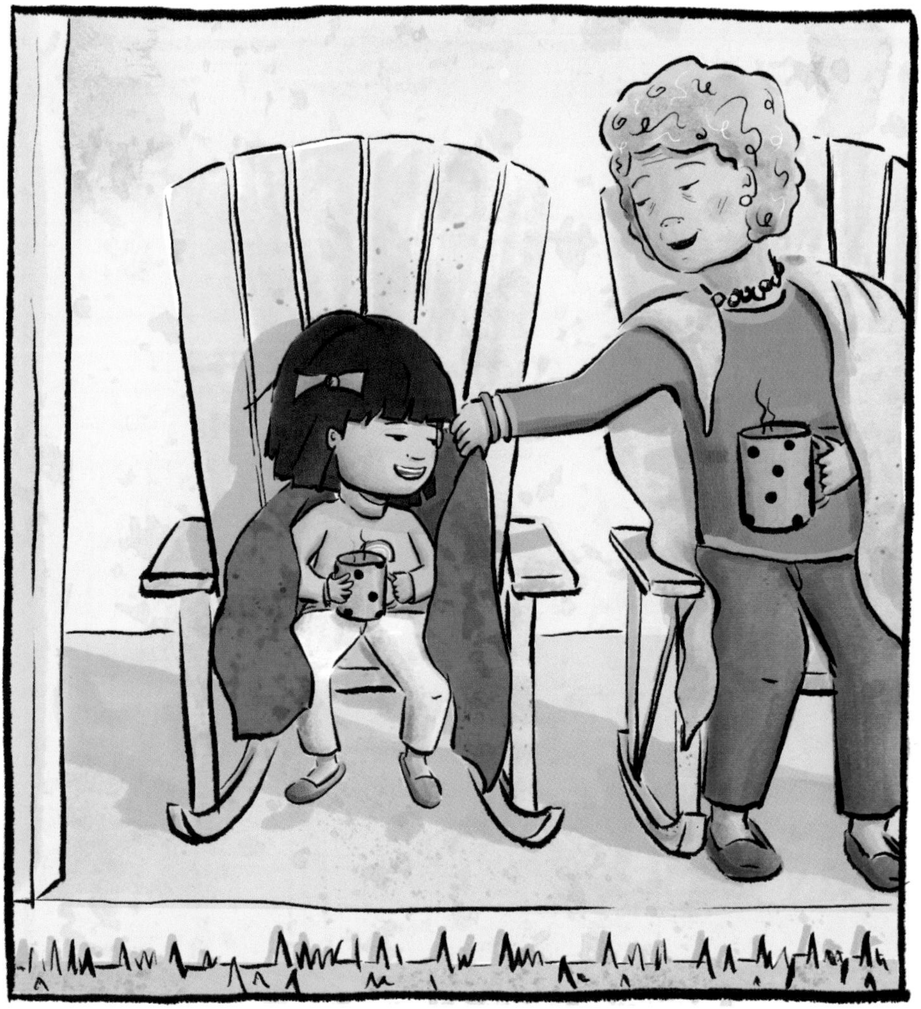

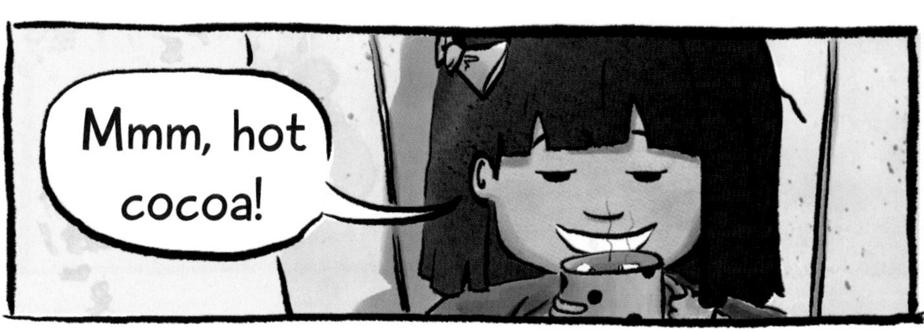
Mmm, hot cocoa!

One afternoon the wind makes Geraldine feel extra chilly.

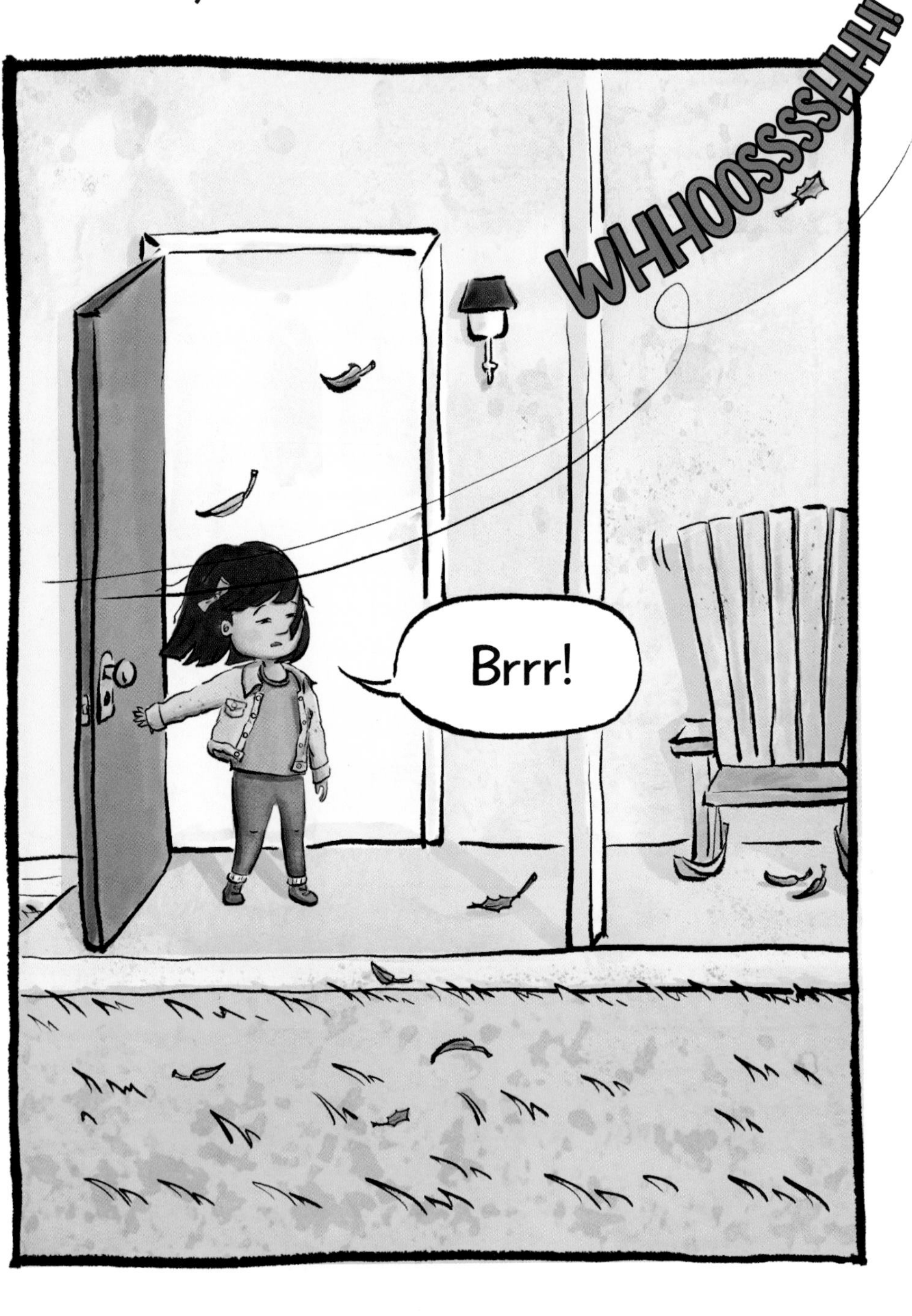
WHHOOSSSSHH!
Brrr!

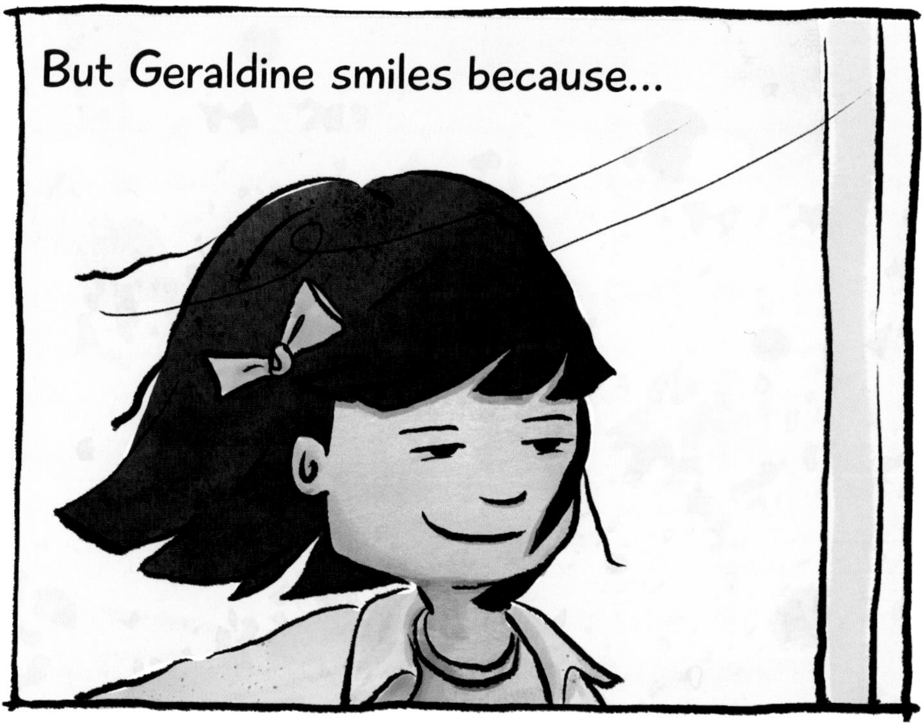
But Geraldine smiles because...

...do you know what else she adores?

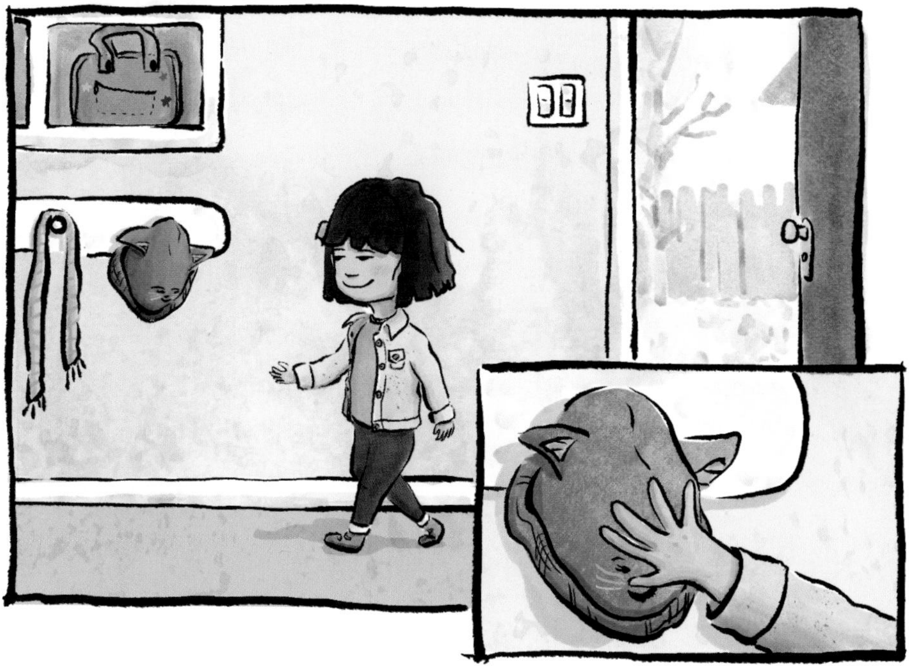

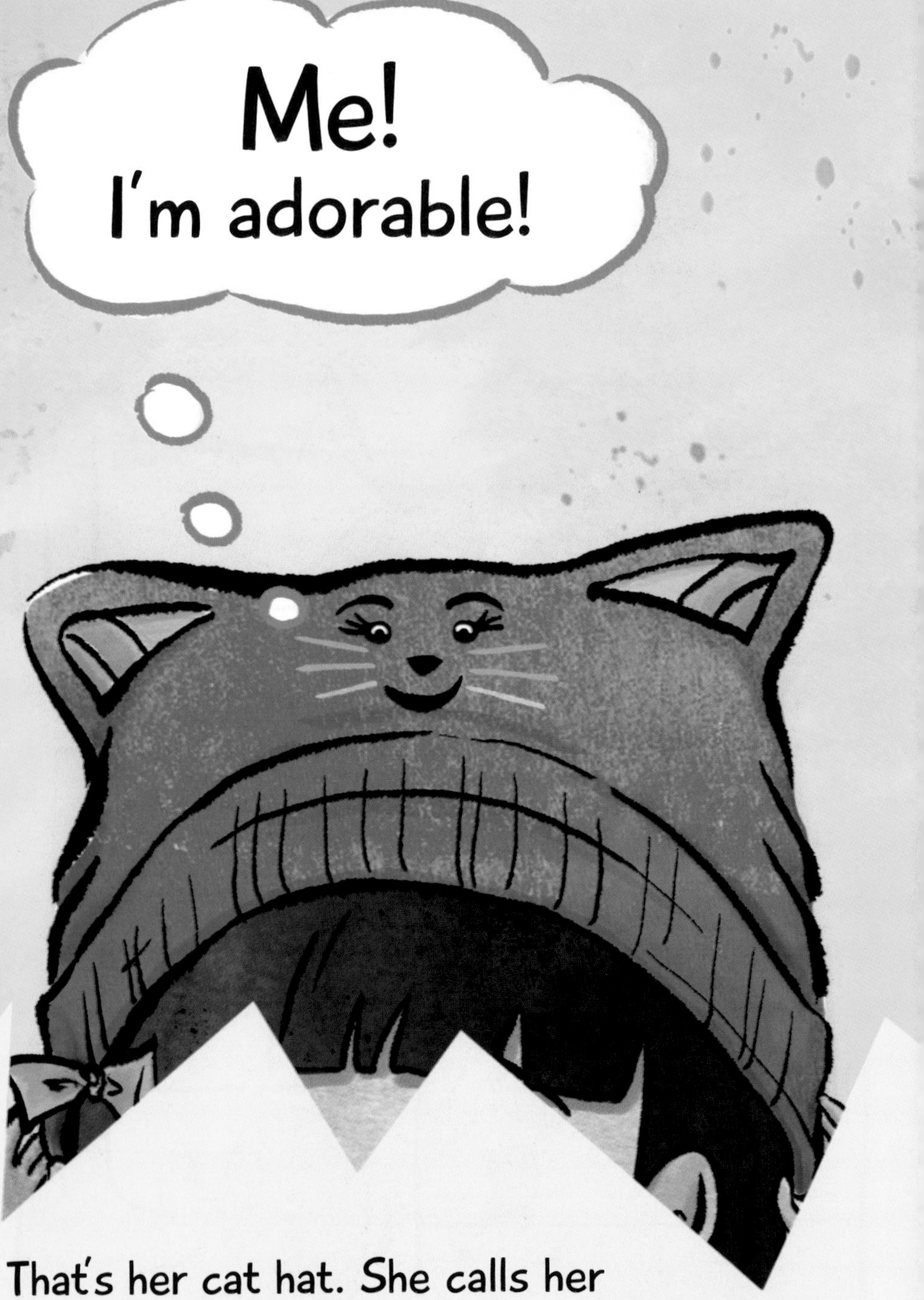
Me!
I'm adorable!

That's her cat hat. She calls her Mao Maotz (said like this: mow MOW-tzz).

Her hat has darling ears and whiskers.

Best of all, I keep Geraldine's head warm!

Geraldine thinks her hat is...

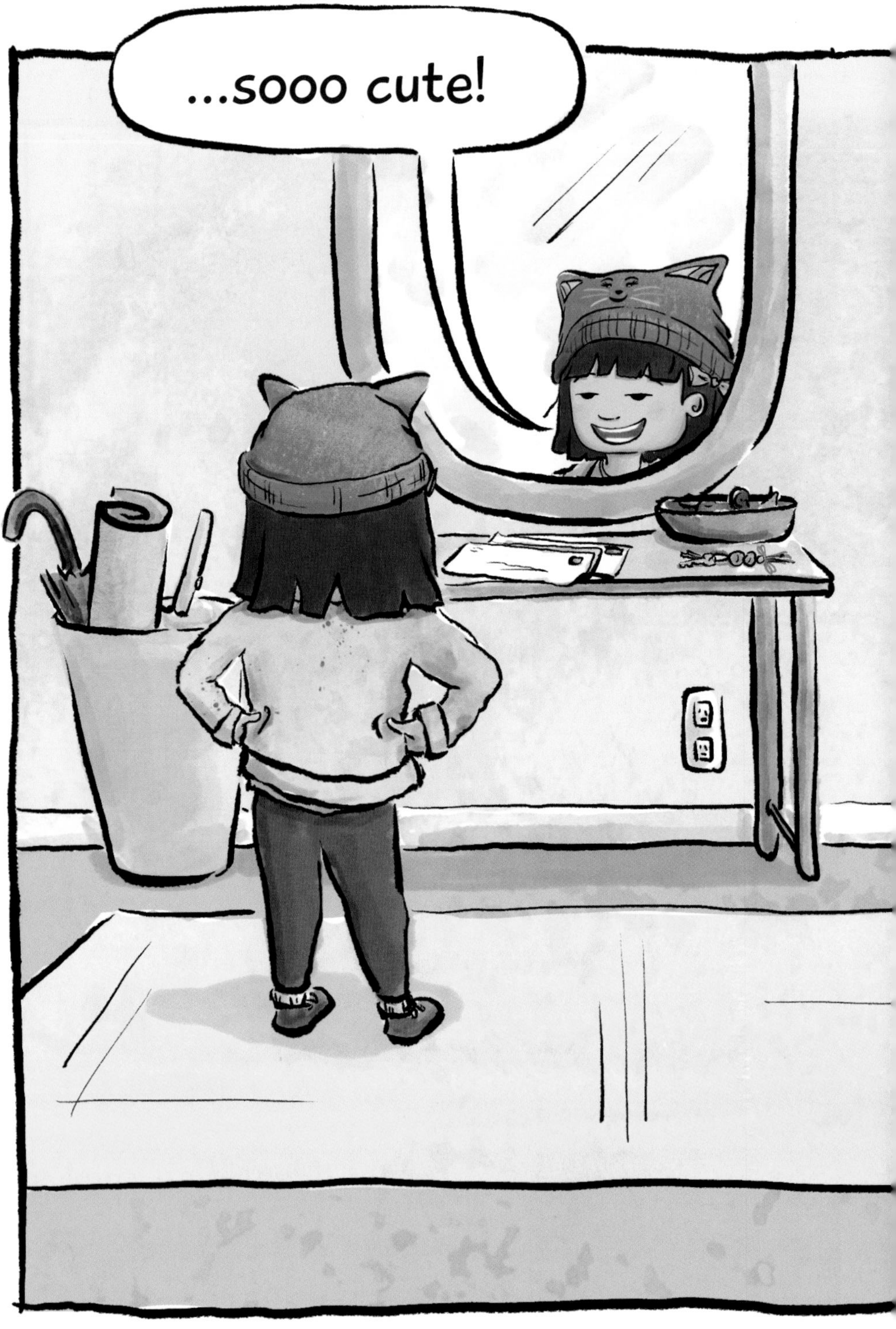
...sooo cute!

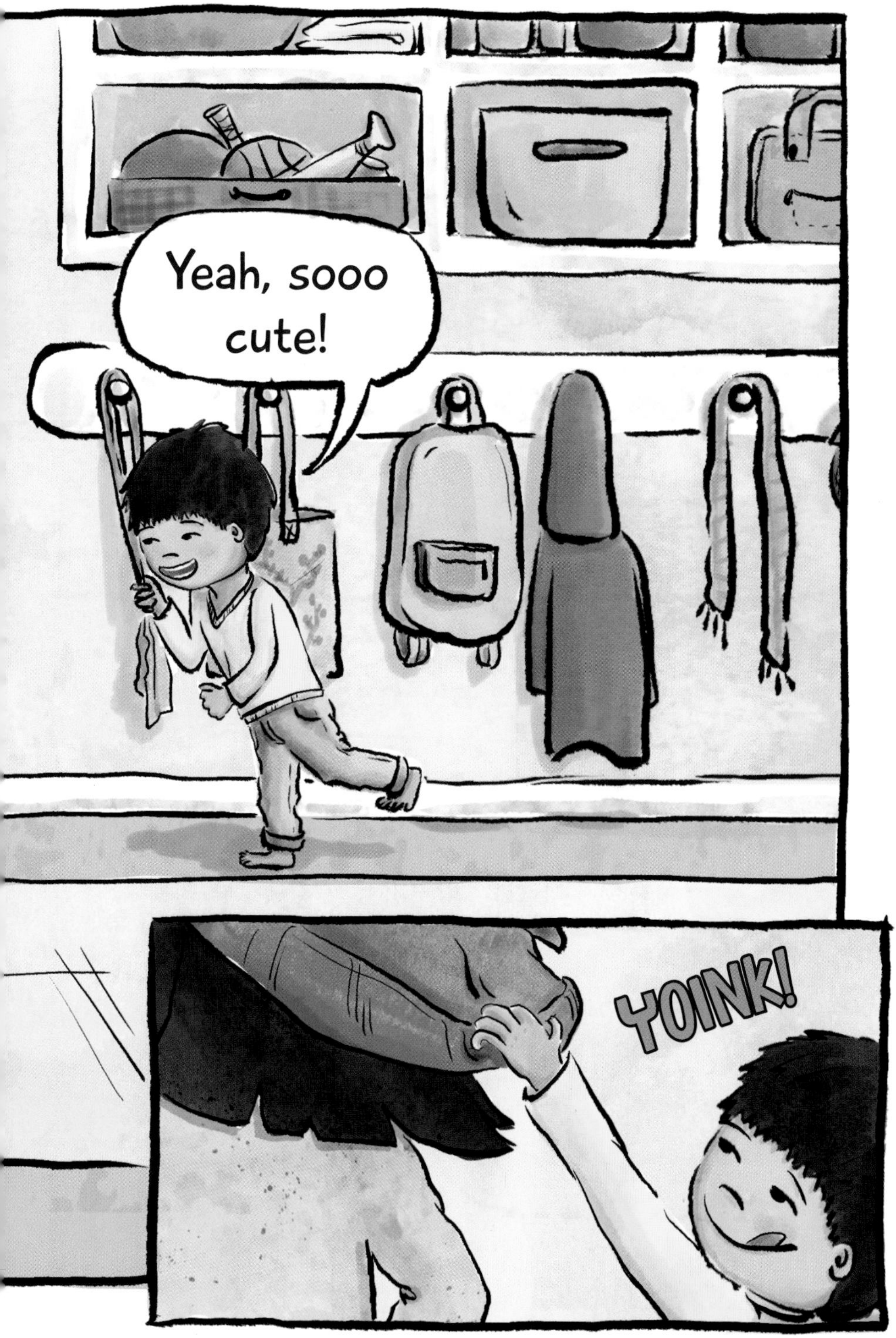
Yeah, sooo cute!
YOINK!

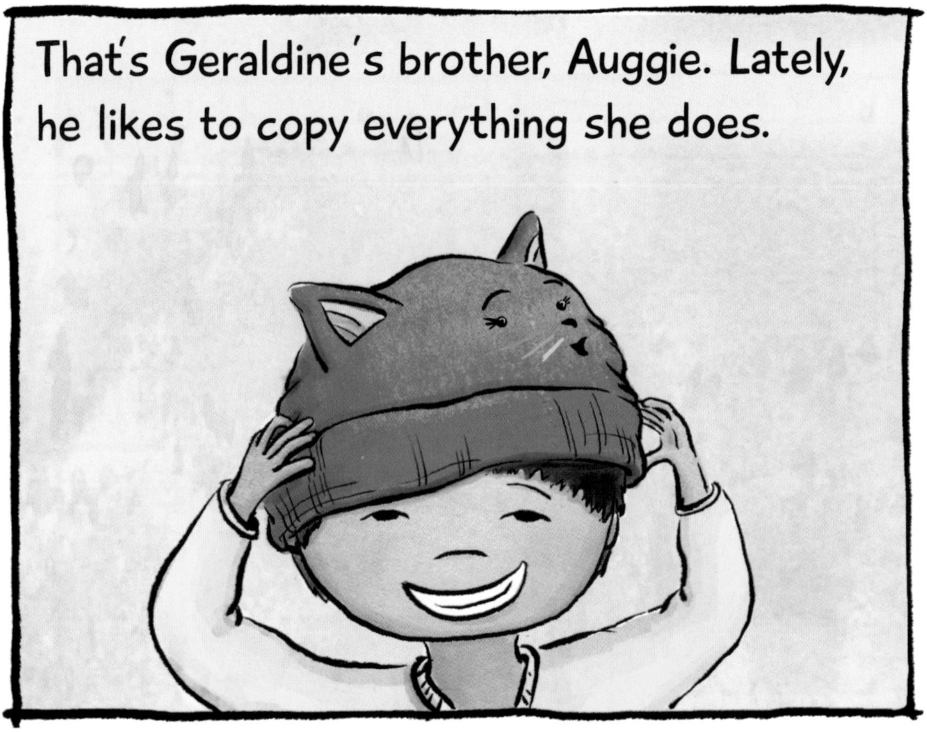
That's Geraldine's brother, Auggie. Lately, he likes to copy everything she does.

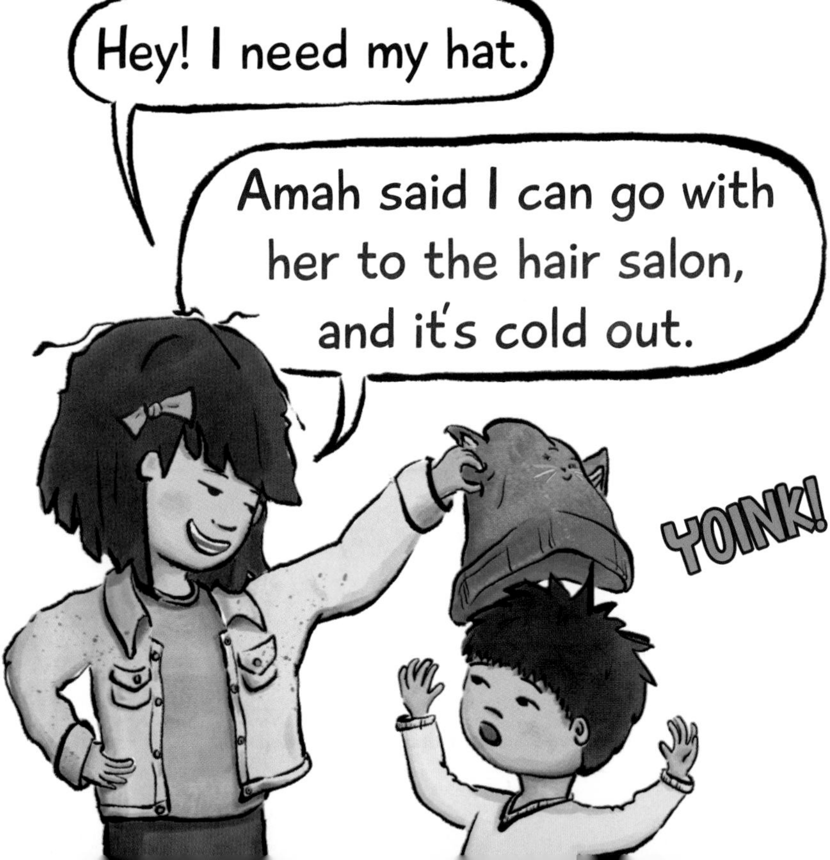
Hey! I need my hat.
Amah said I can go with her to the hair salon, and it's cold out.
YOINK!

Auggie pouts.

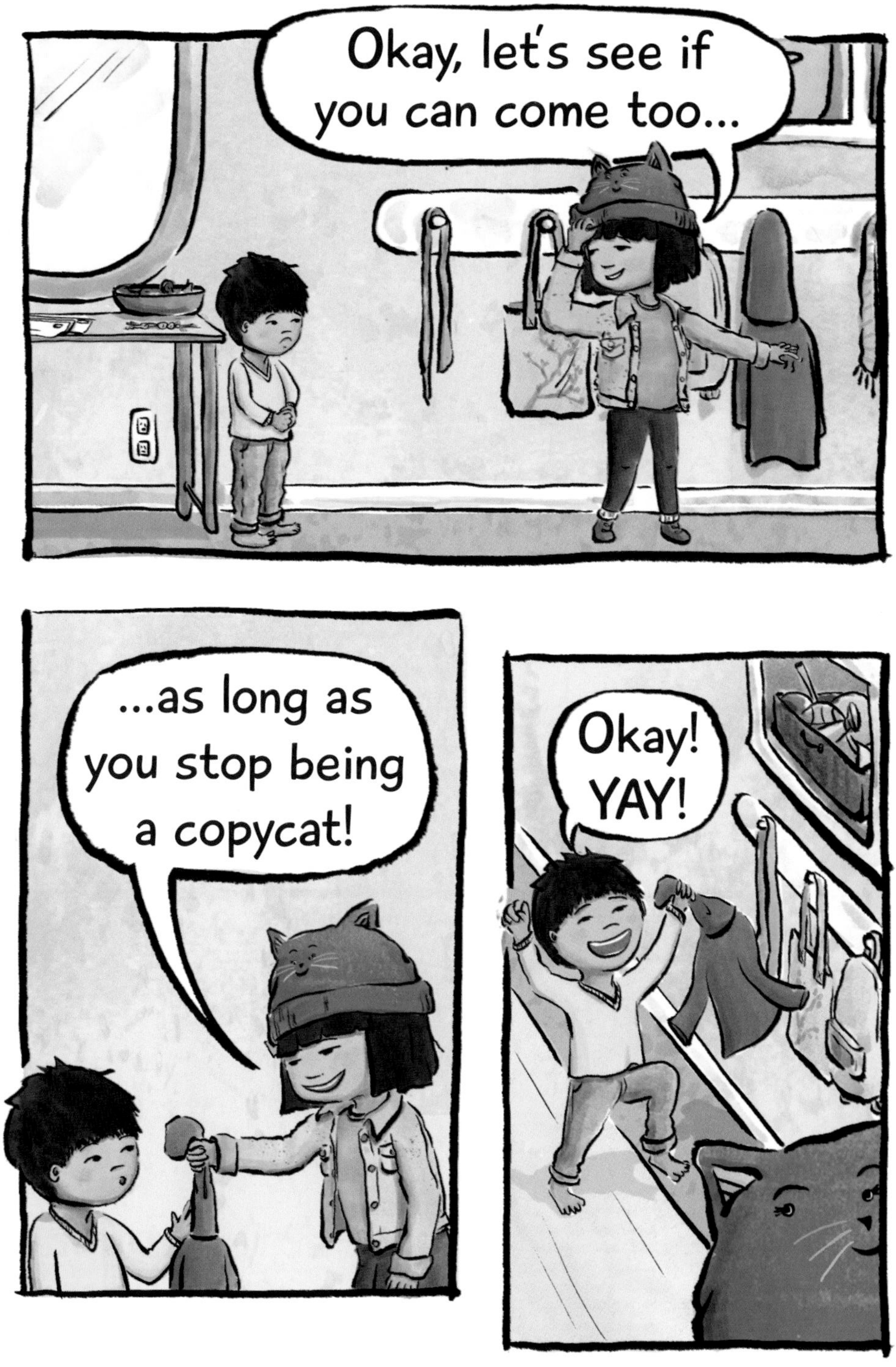
Okay, let's see if you can come too...
...as long as you stop being a copycat!
Okay! YAY!

At the salon the hairstylist compliments Geraldine.

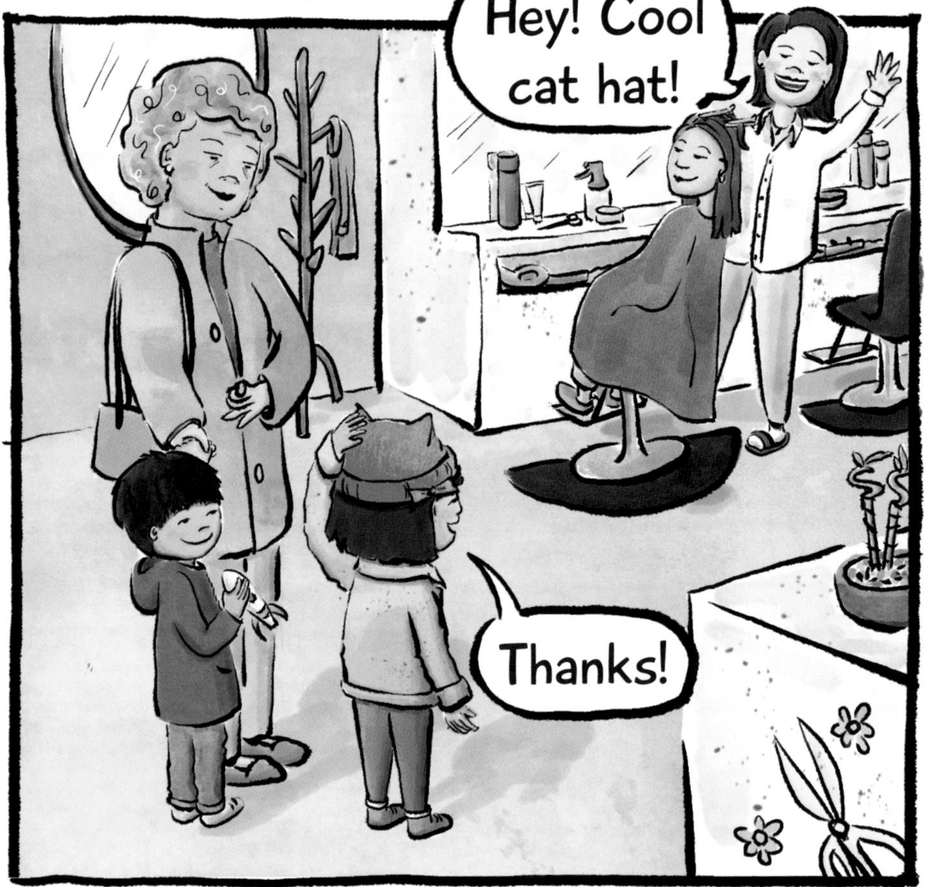
Hey! Cool cat hat!
Thanks!

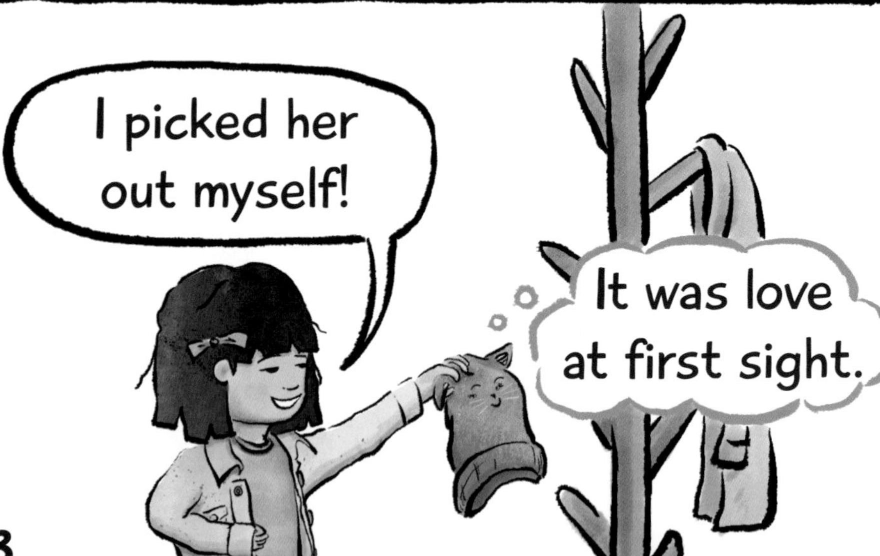
I picked her out myself!
It was love at first sight.

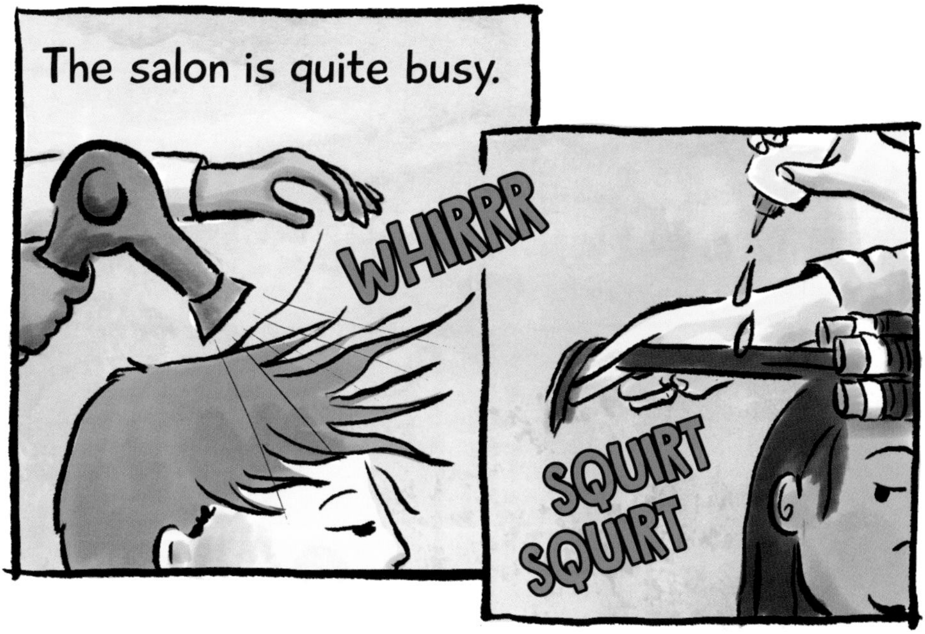
The salon is quite busy.
WHIRRR
SQUIRT
SQUIRT

So, Geraldine and Auggie find a place to sit during Amah's haircut.

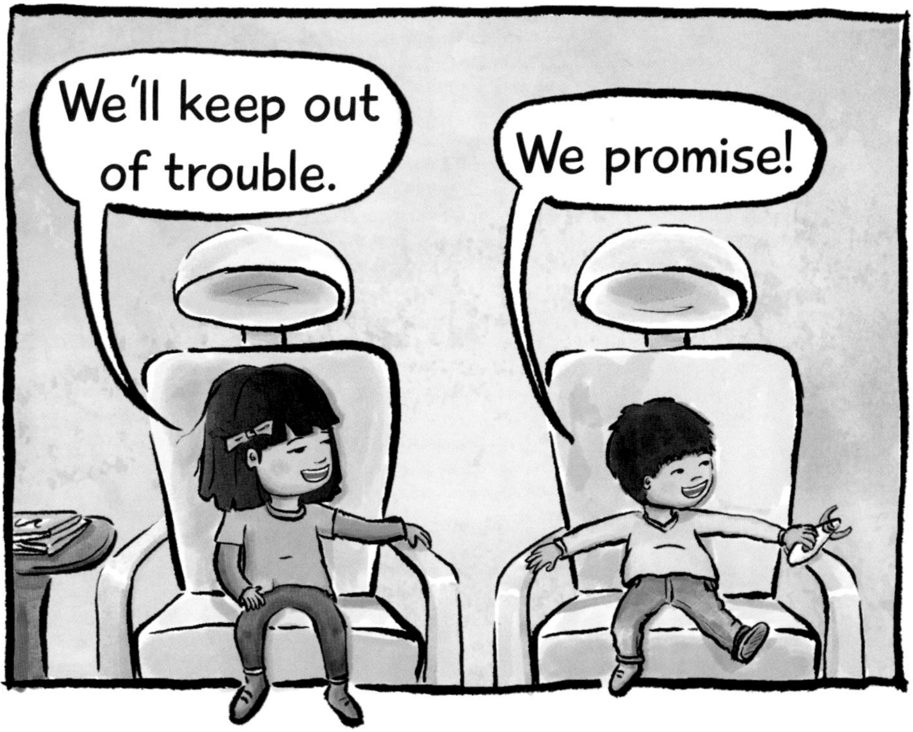
We'll keep out of trouble.
We promise!

Chapter Two

As they wait, Auggie pretends to be the hairstylist.

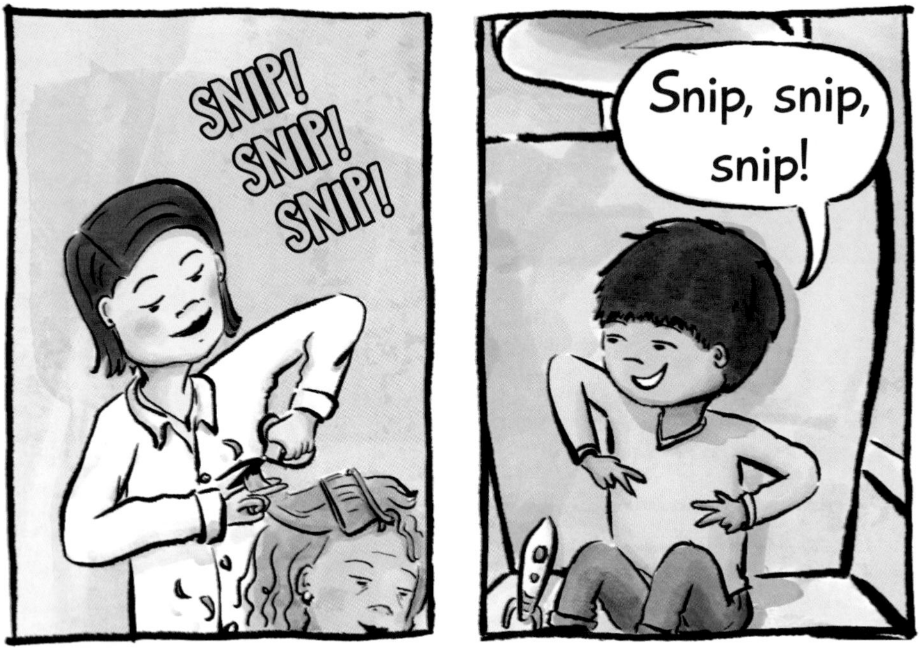
SNIP!
SNIP!
SNIP!
Snip, snip,
snip!

Meanwhile, Geraldine looks at photos of all kinds of hair.

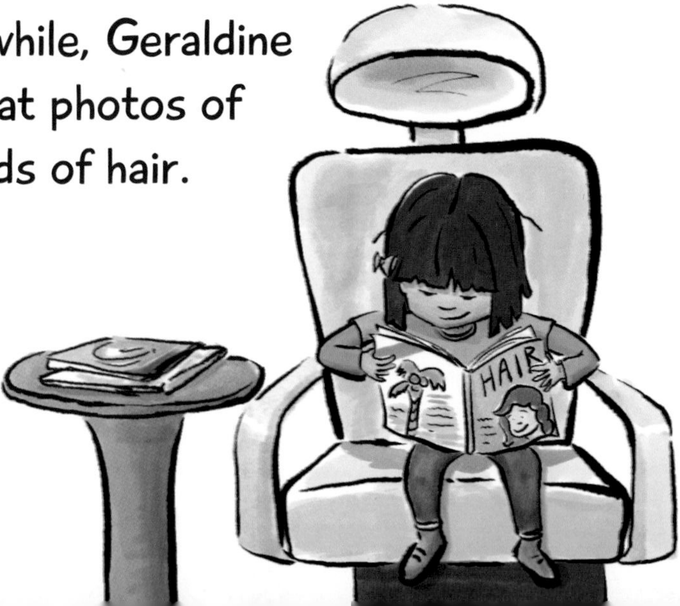
HAIR

She sees
wavy hair like
Amah's.

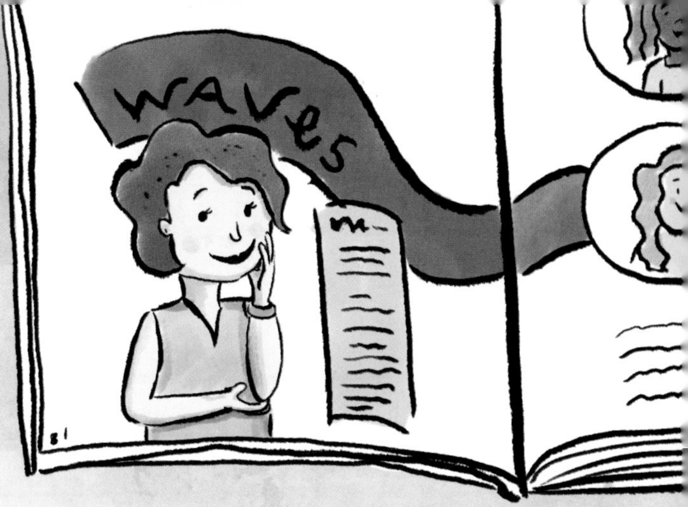
WAVES

There's also hair that's

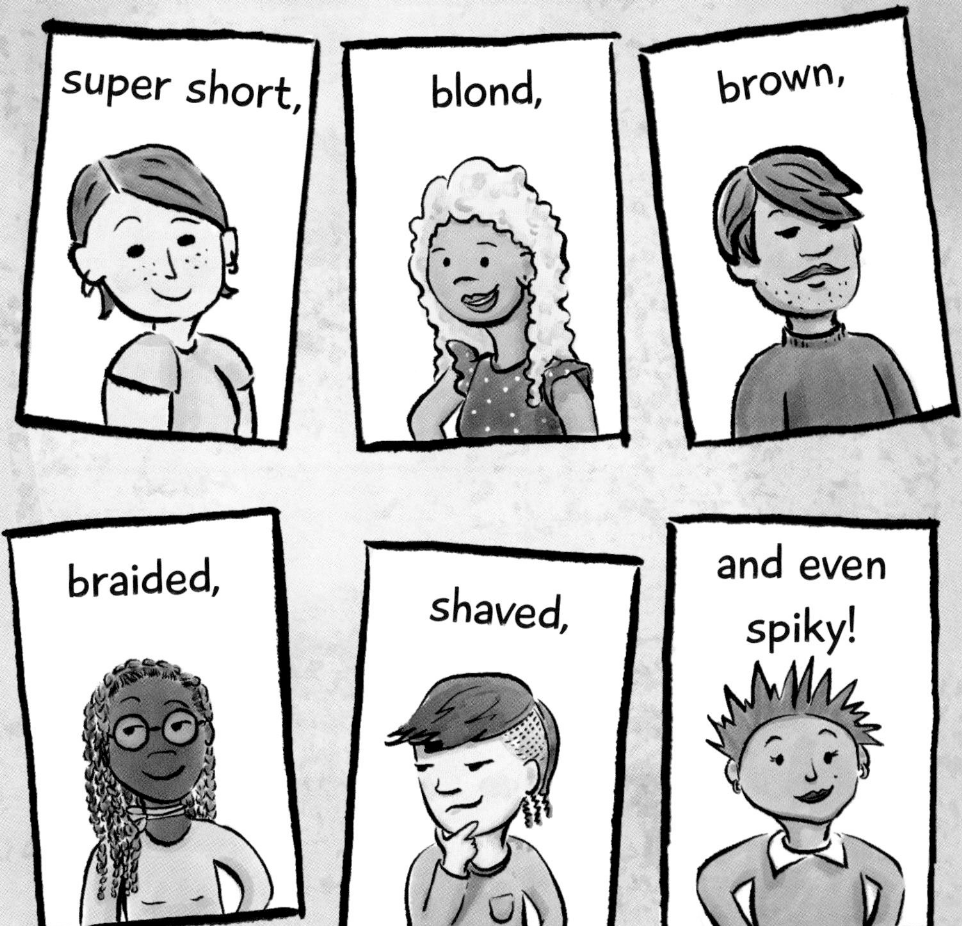
super short,
blond,
brown,
braided,
shaved,
and even
spiky!

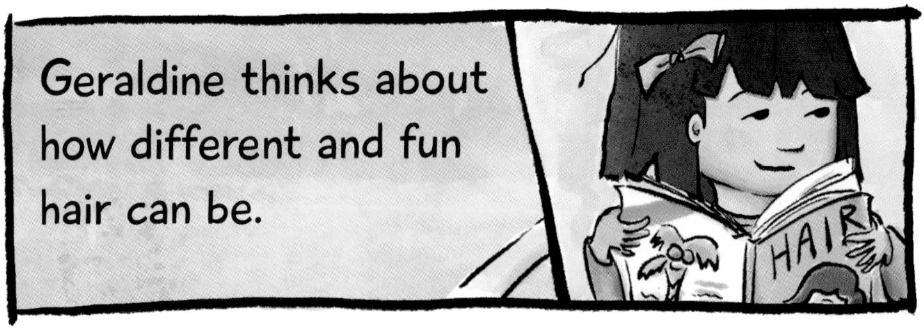
Geraldine thinks about how different and fun hair can be.
HAIR

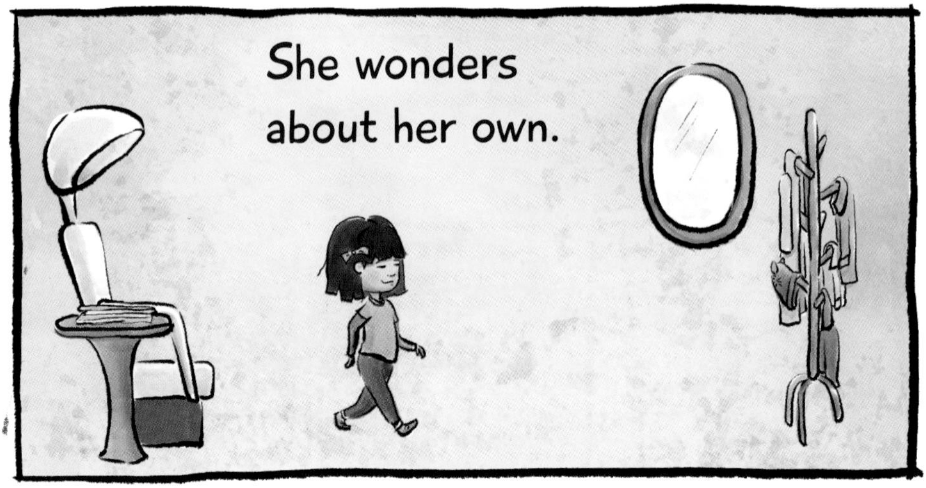
She wonders about her own.

It's straight.

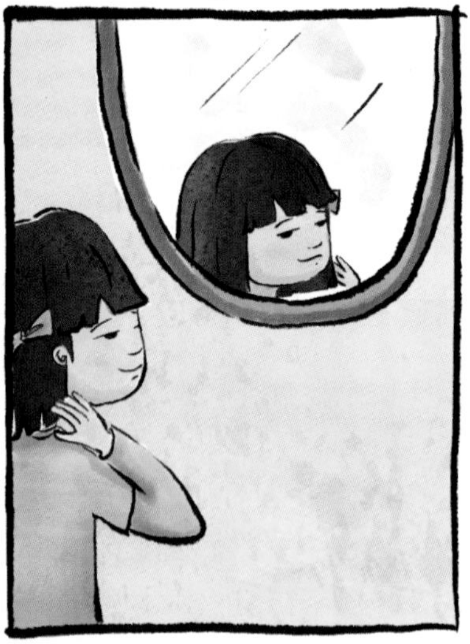

It's black. And it's...

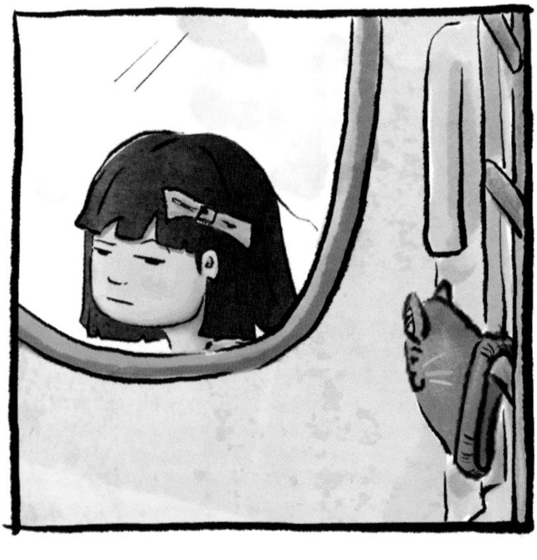

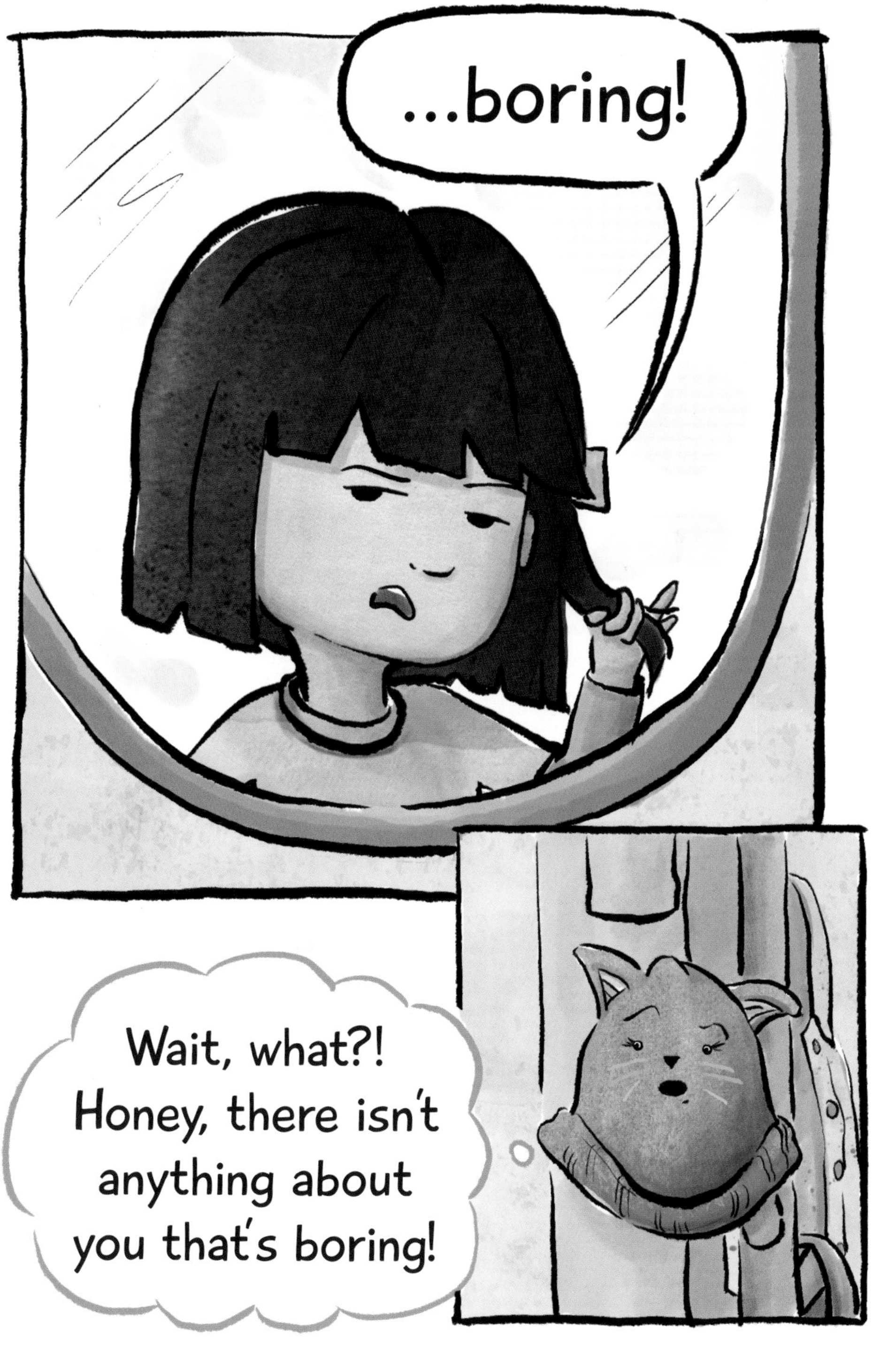
...boring!
Wait, what?! Honey, there isn't anything about you that's boring!

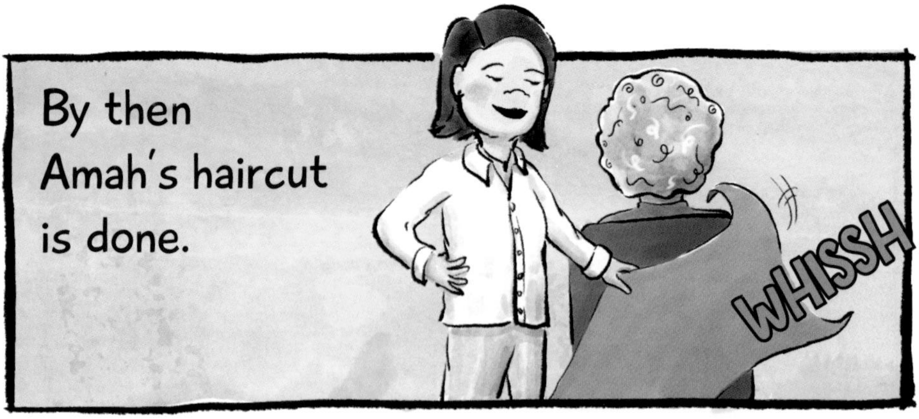
By then
Amah's haircut
is done.
WHISSH

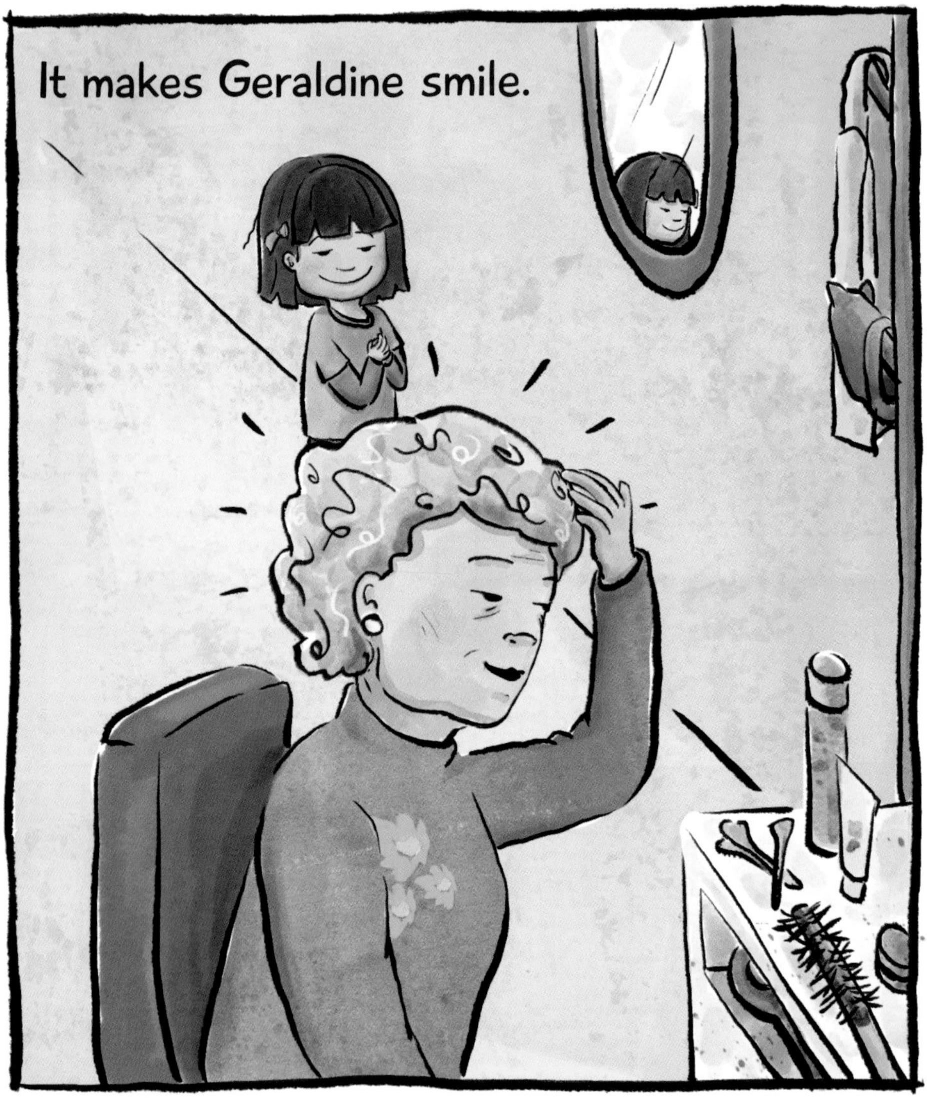
It makes Geraldine smile.

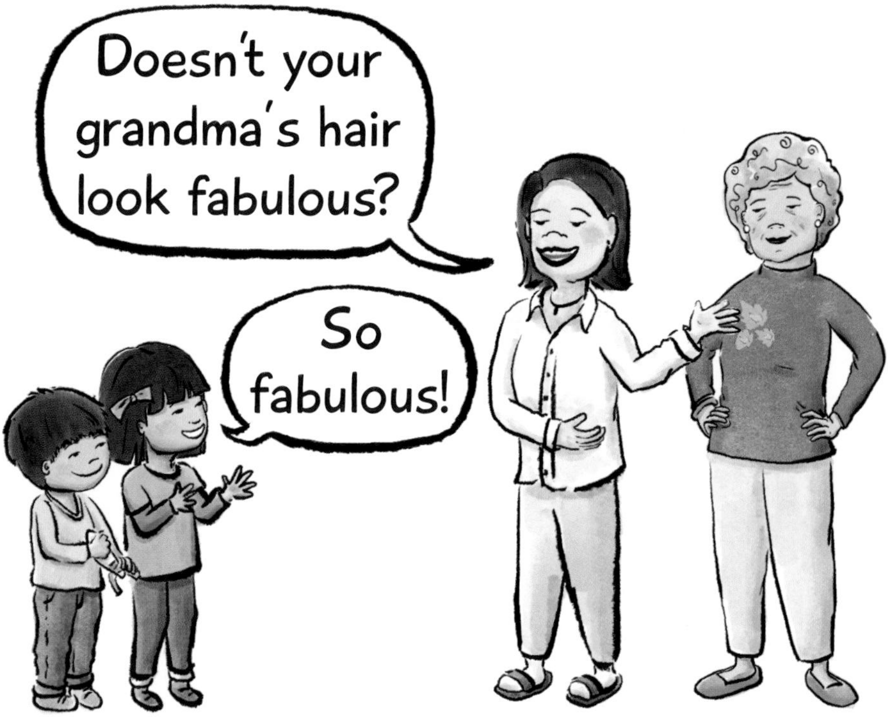
Doesn't your grandma's hair look fabulous?
So fabulous!

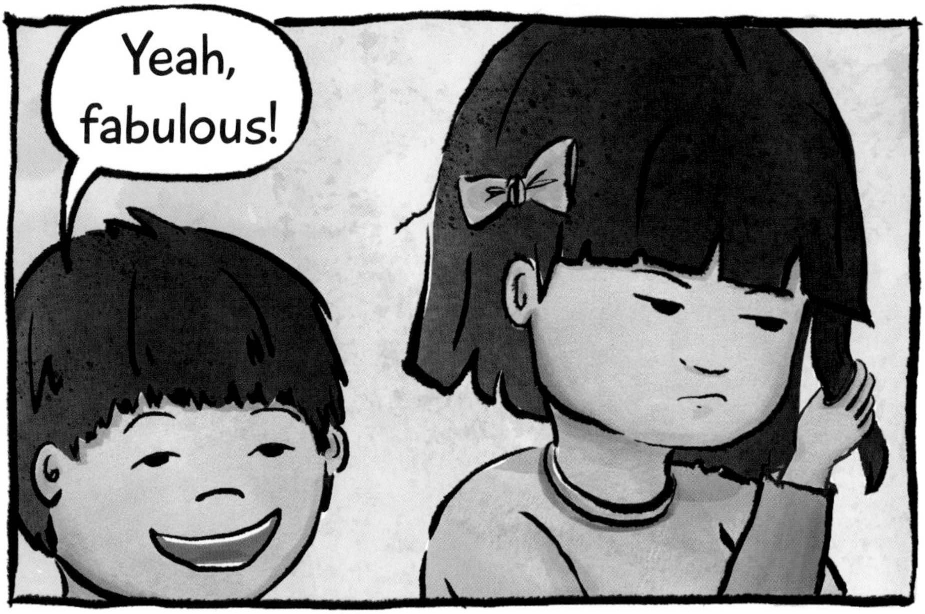
Yeah, fabulous!

Geraldine frowns, and it's not because Auggie's copying her.

The next day is chilly again, although the bus is quite warm.

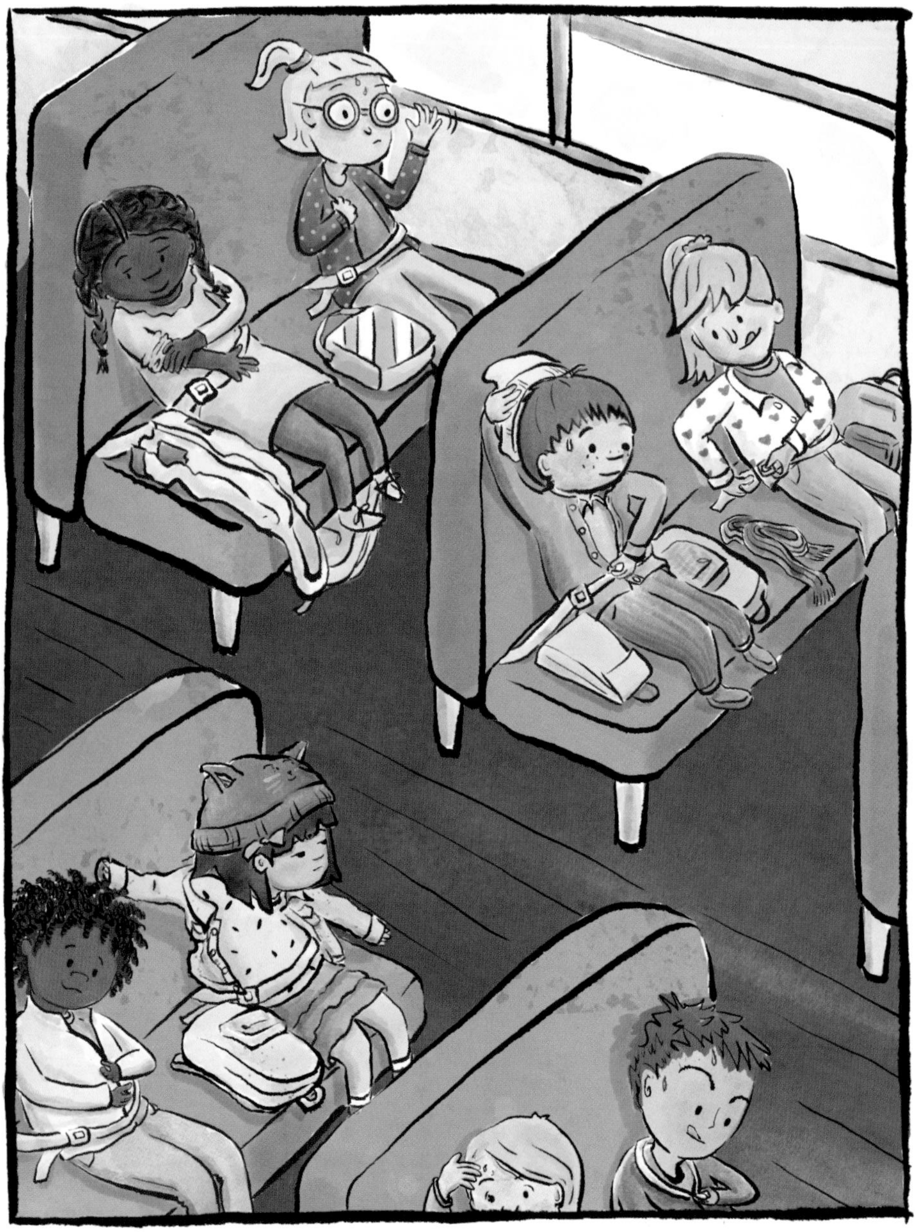

Even then, Geraldine keeps Mao Maotz on.

She asks her friend Deven,

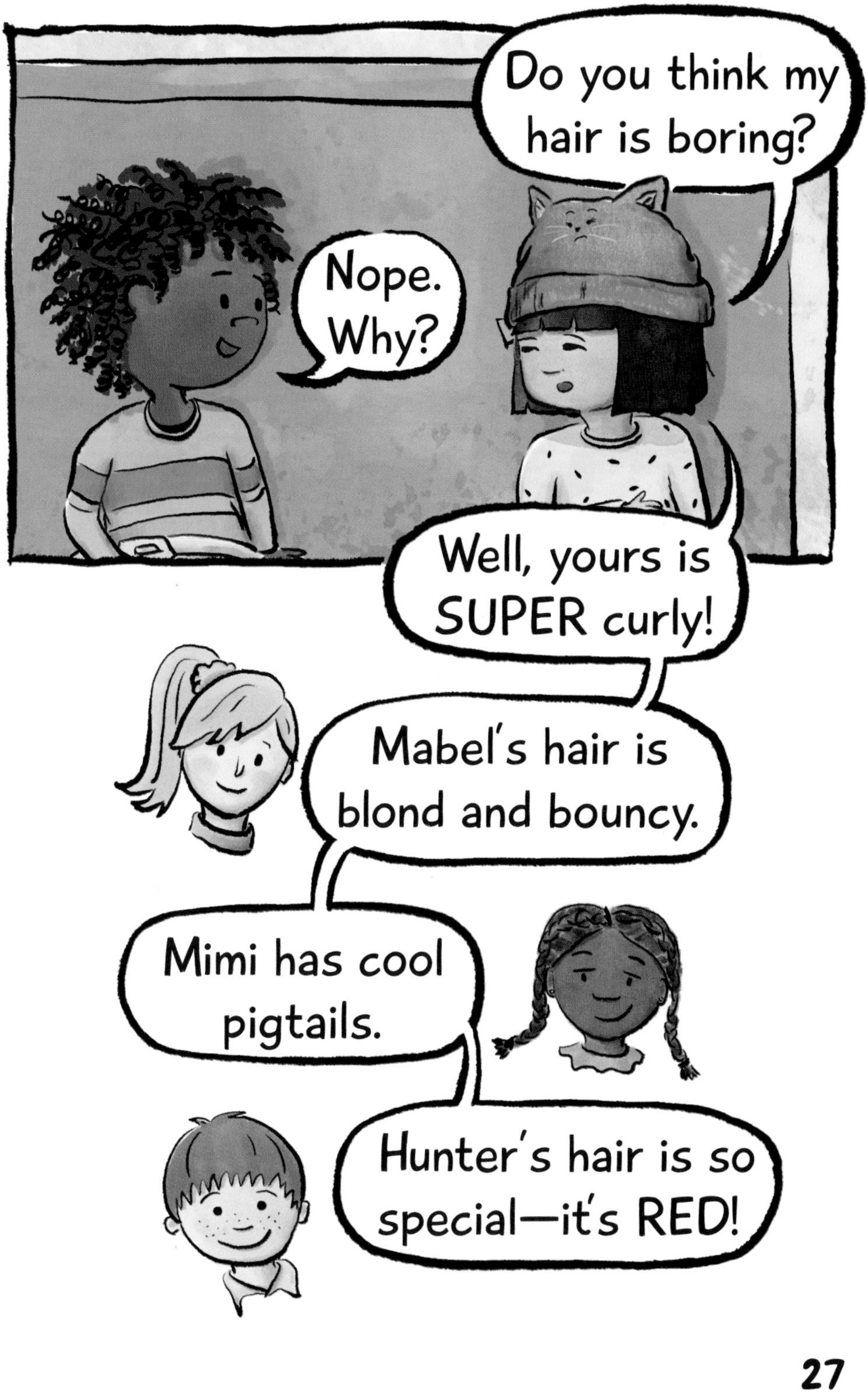
Do you think my hair is boring?
Nope. Why?
Well, yours is SUPER curly!
Mabel's hair is blond and bouncy.
Mimi has cool pigtails.
Hunter's hair is so special—it's RED!

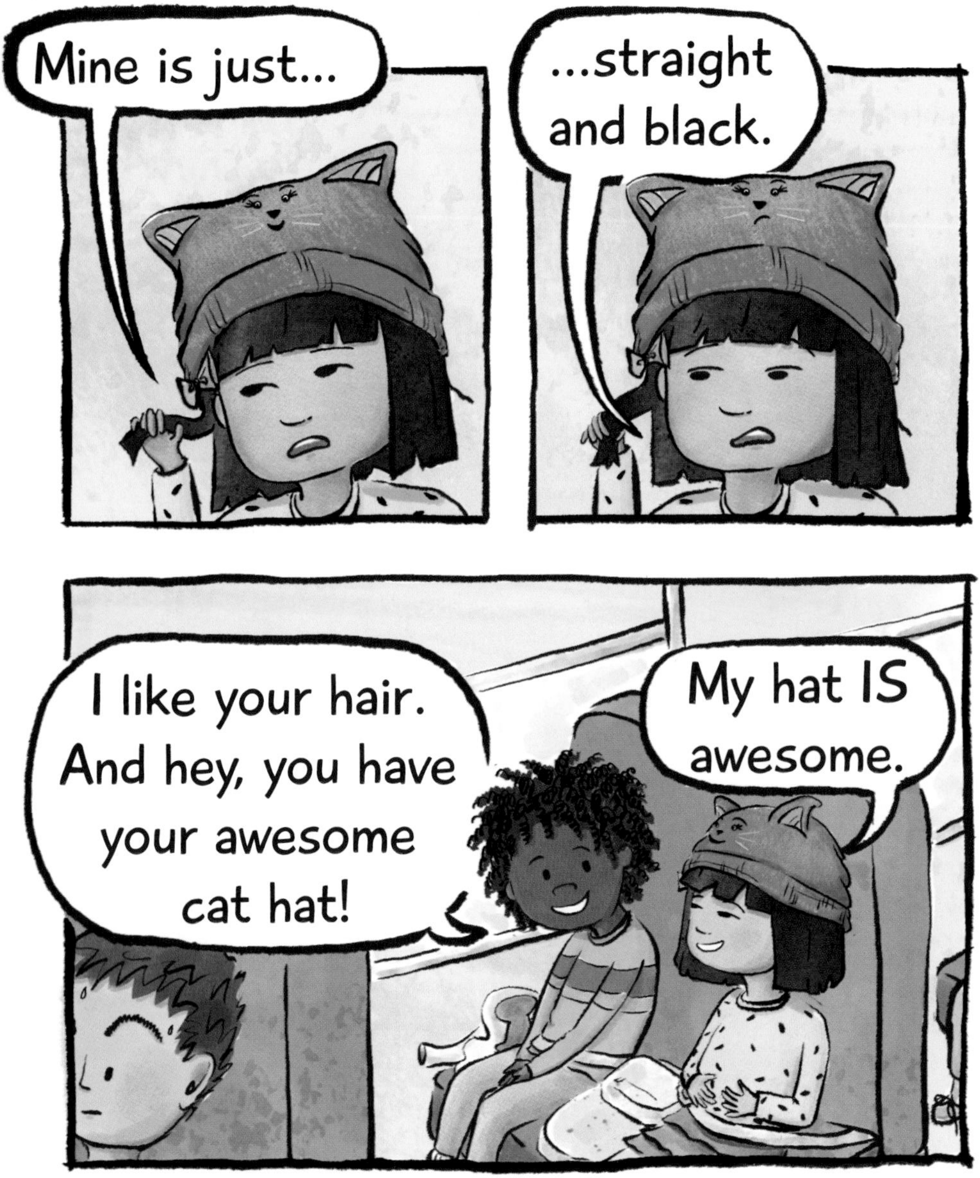
Mine is just...
...straight and black.
I like your hair. And hey, you have your awesome cat hat!
My hat IS awesome.

But Geraldine's still unsure about her hair.

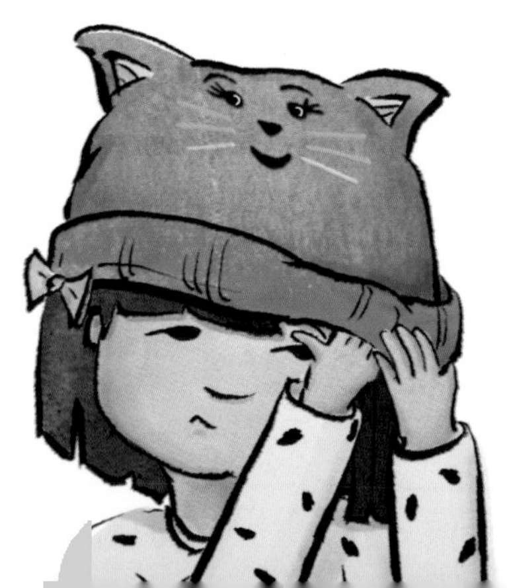

Mao Maotz stays on Geraldine's head as school starts...

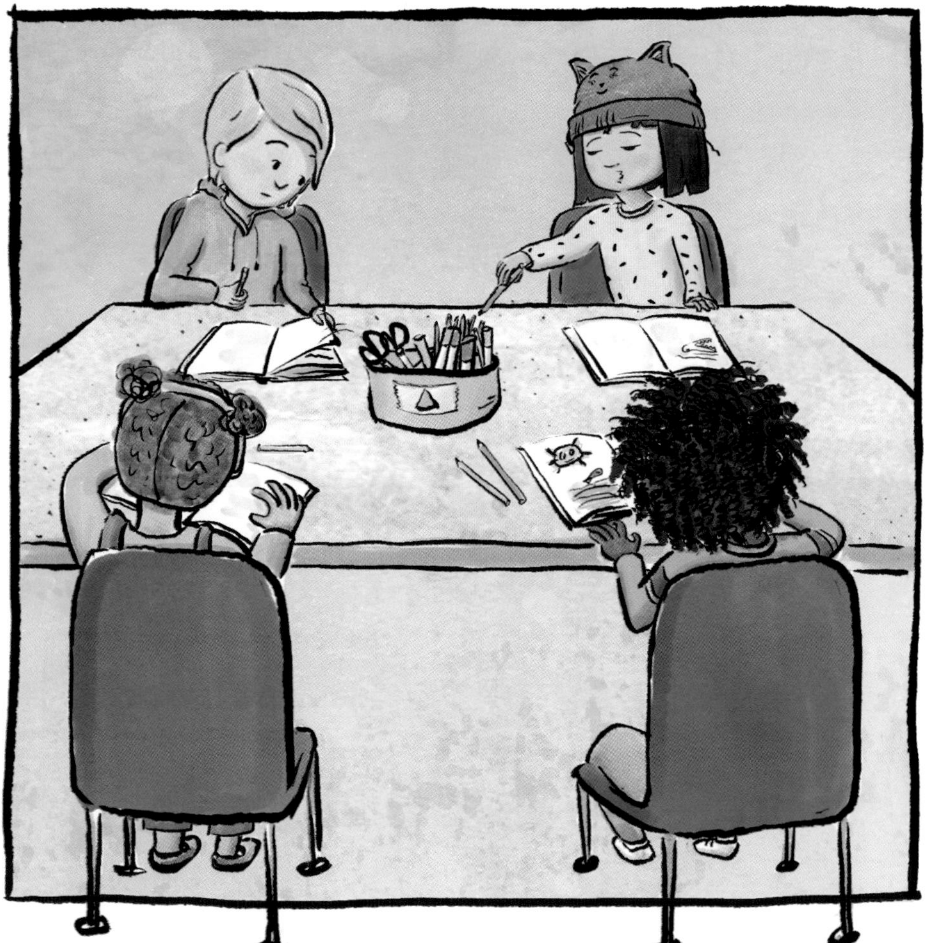

...even though there's a strict rule:

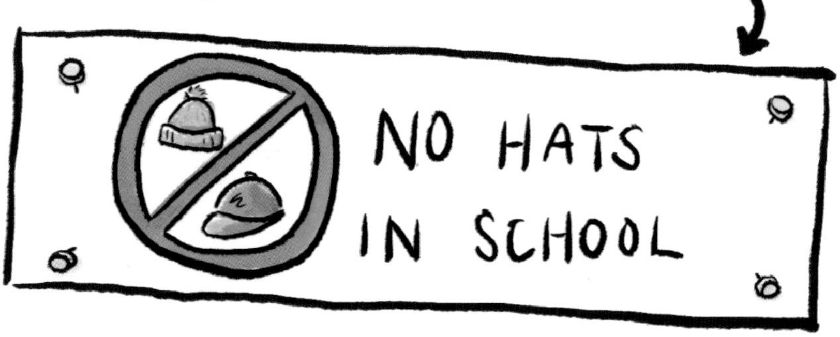
NO HATS
IN SCHOOL

Nico notices right away.

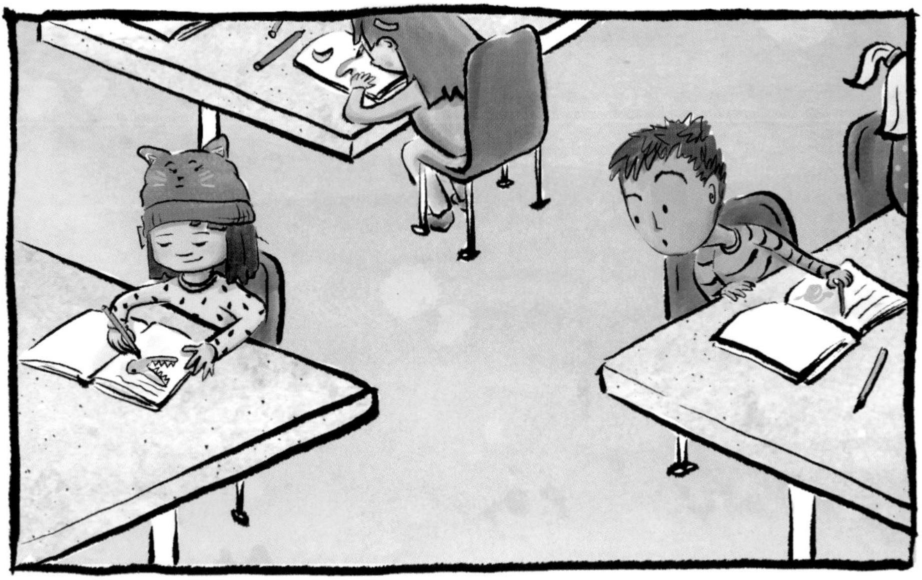

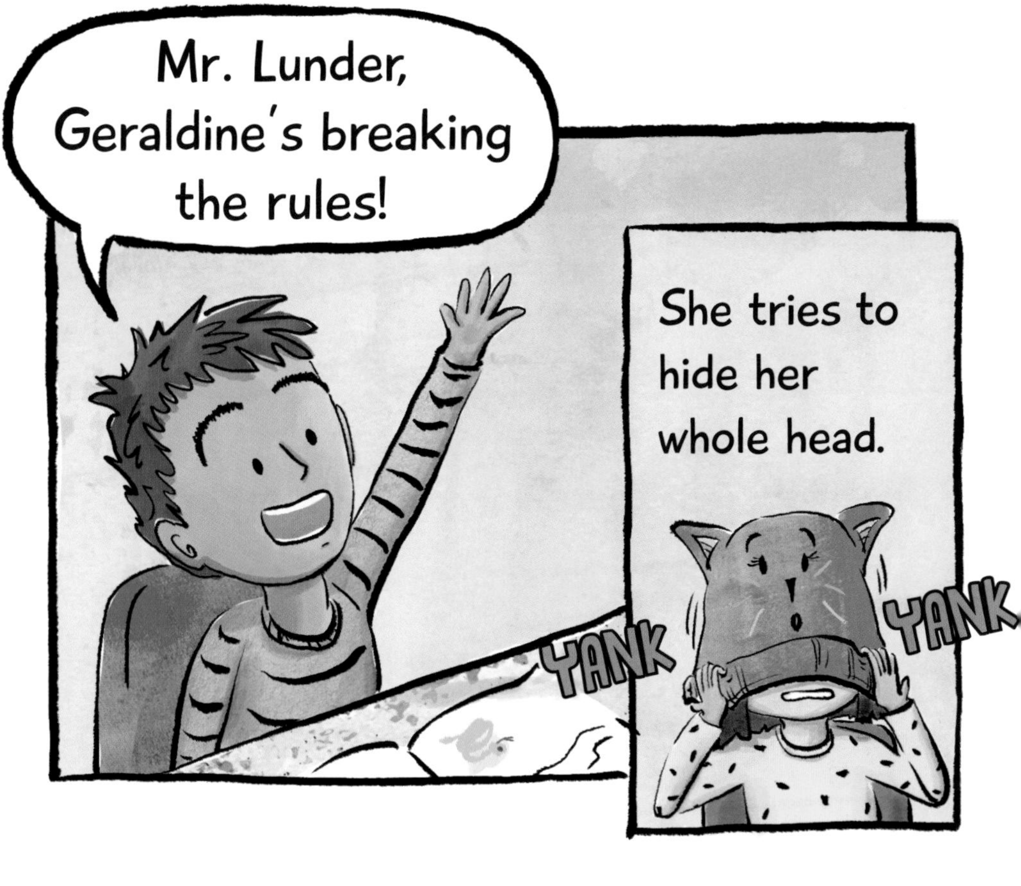
Mr. Lunder, Geraldine's breaking the rules!
She tries to hide her whole head.
YANK
YANK

But she can still hear Mr. Lunder as he says,

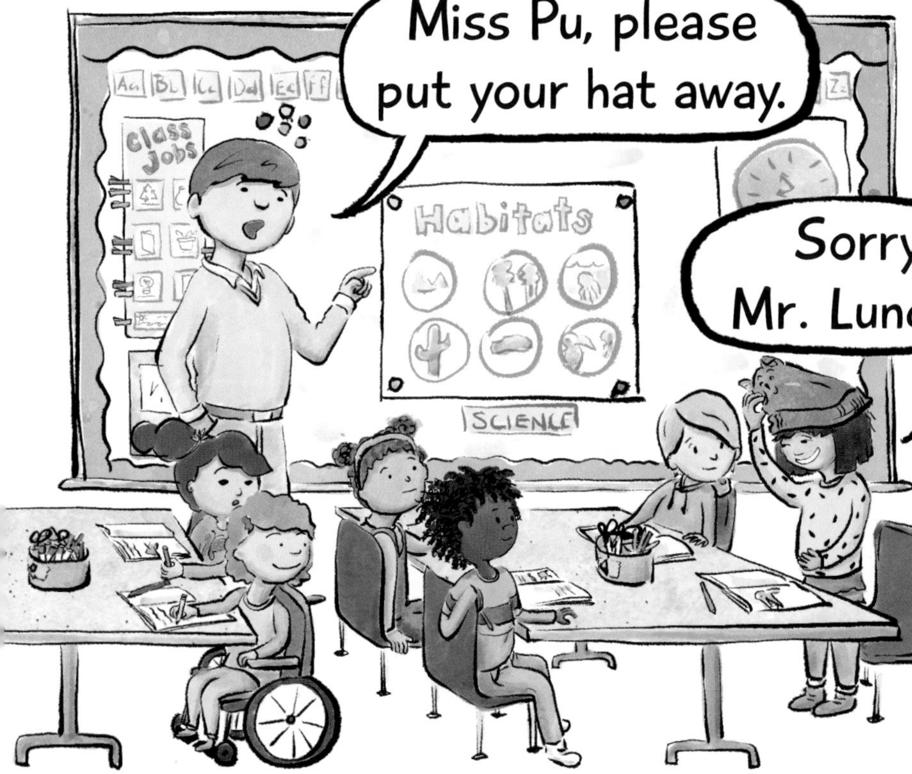
Miss Pu, please put your hat away.
Class Jobs
Habitats
SCIENCE
Sorry, Mr. Lunder.

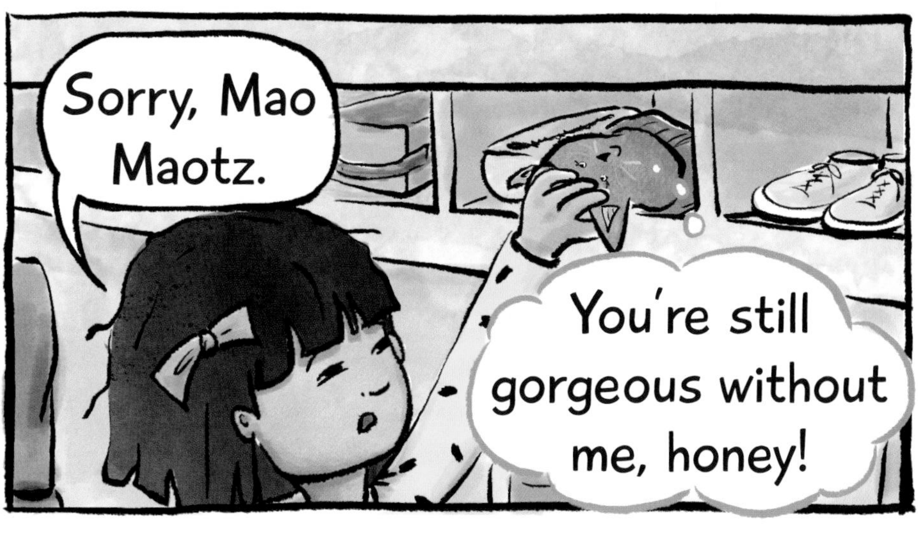
Sorry, Mao Maotz.
You're still gorgeous without me, honey!

As Geraldine returns to her seat, Mr. Lunder reminds the class,

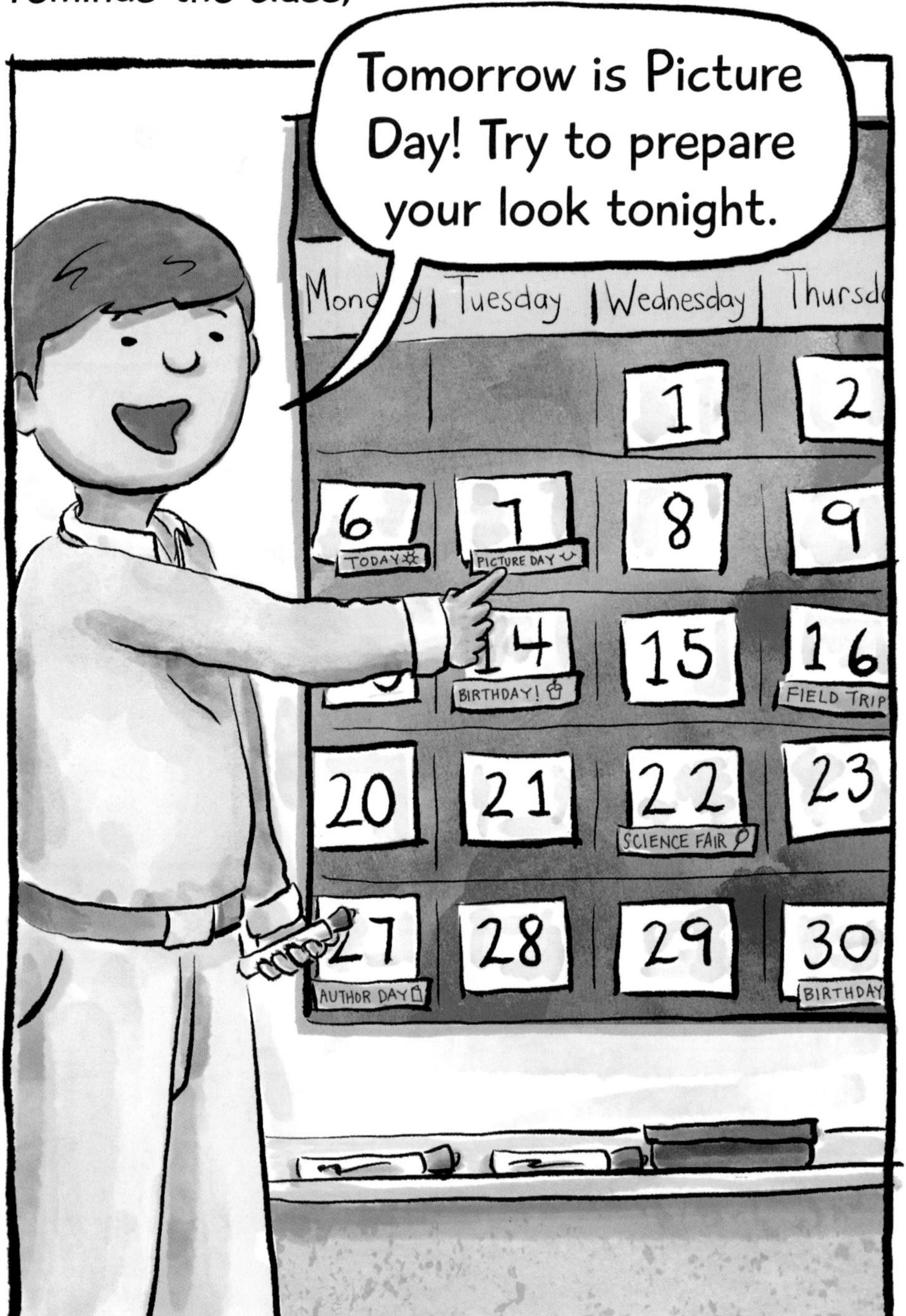
Tomorrow is Picture Day! Try to prepare your look tonight.
Tuesday
Wednesday
1
2
6
TODAY
7
PICTURE DAY
8
9
14
BIRTHDAY!
15
16
FIELD TRIP
20
21
22
SCIENCE FAIR
23
27
AUTHOR DAY
28
29
30
BIRTHDAY

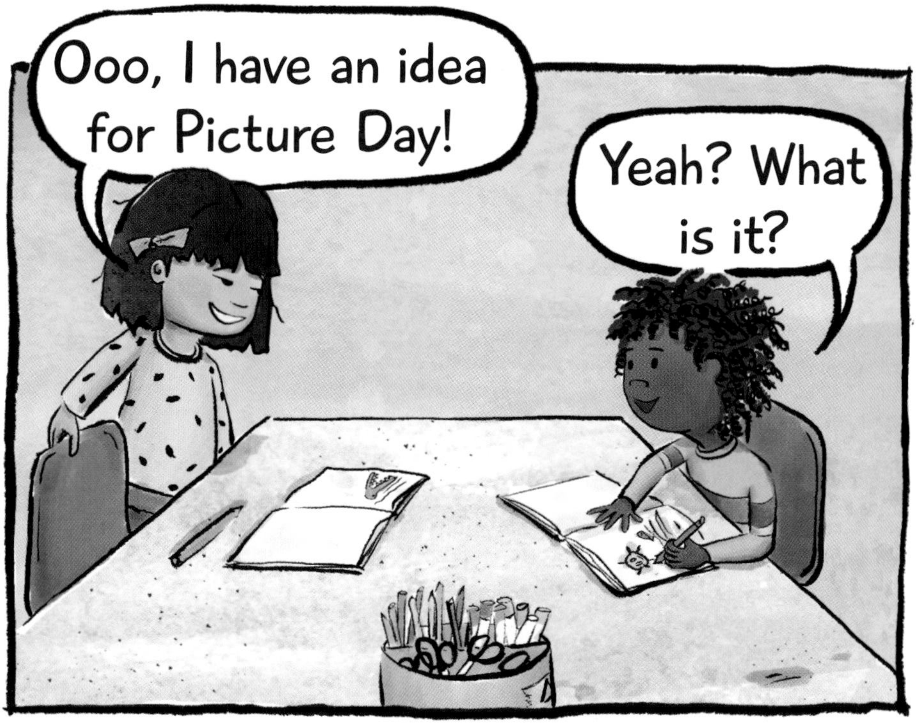
Ooo, I have an idea for Picture Day!
Yeah? What is it?

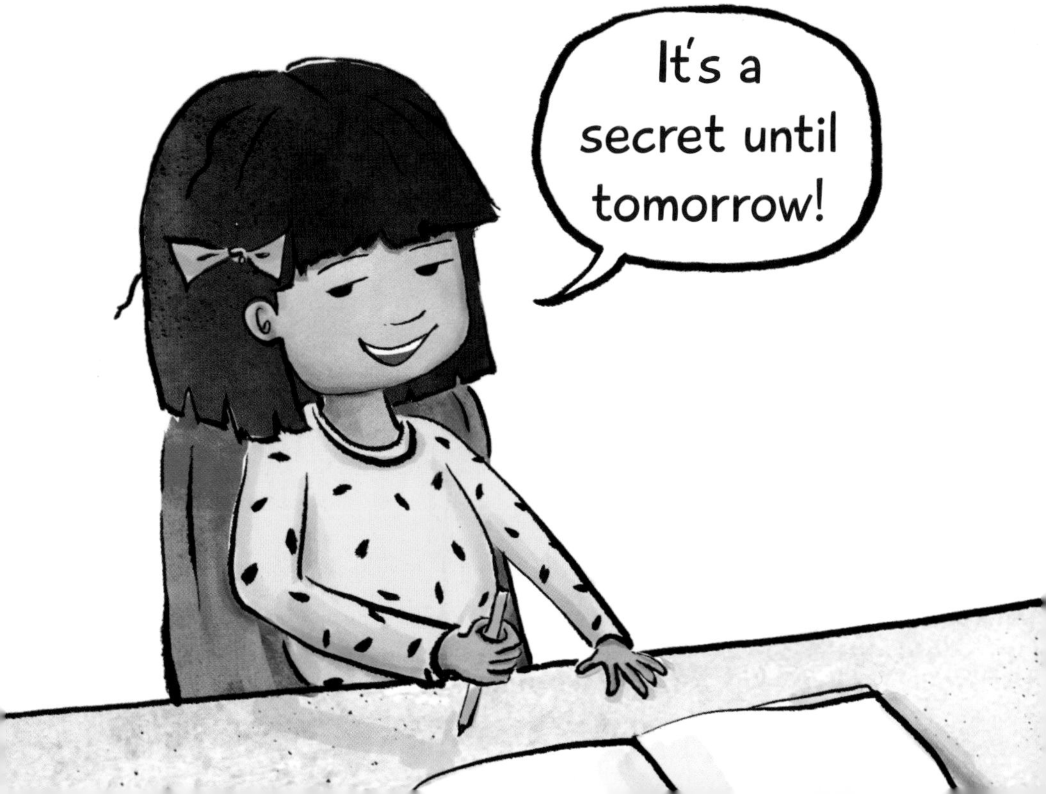
It's a secret until tomorrow!

Chapter Three

When Geraldine gets home, she gathers supplies for her idea.

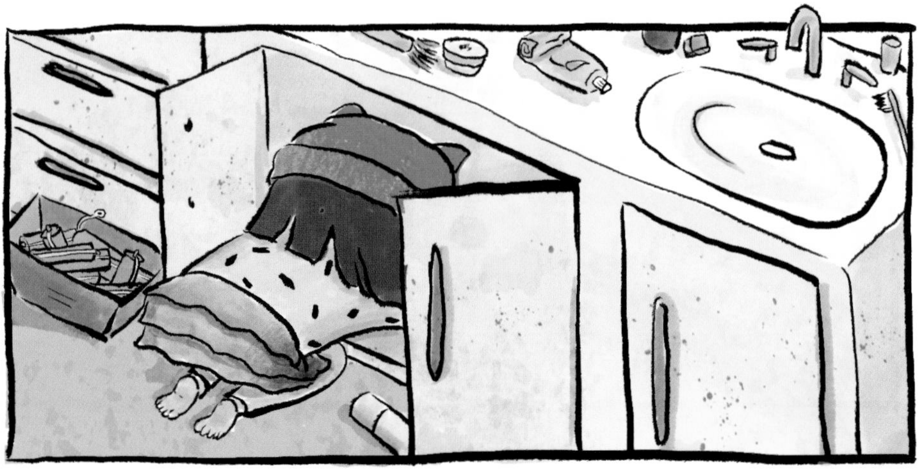

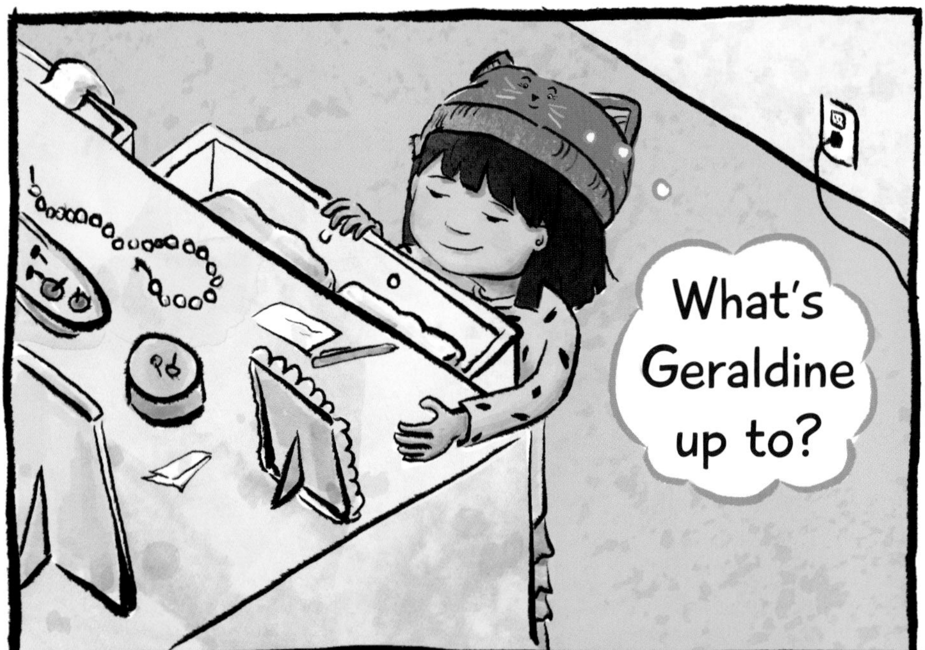
What's Geraldine up to?

Once she's ready, she declares,

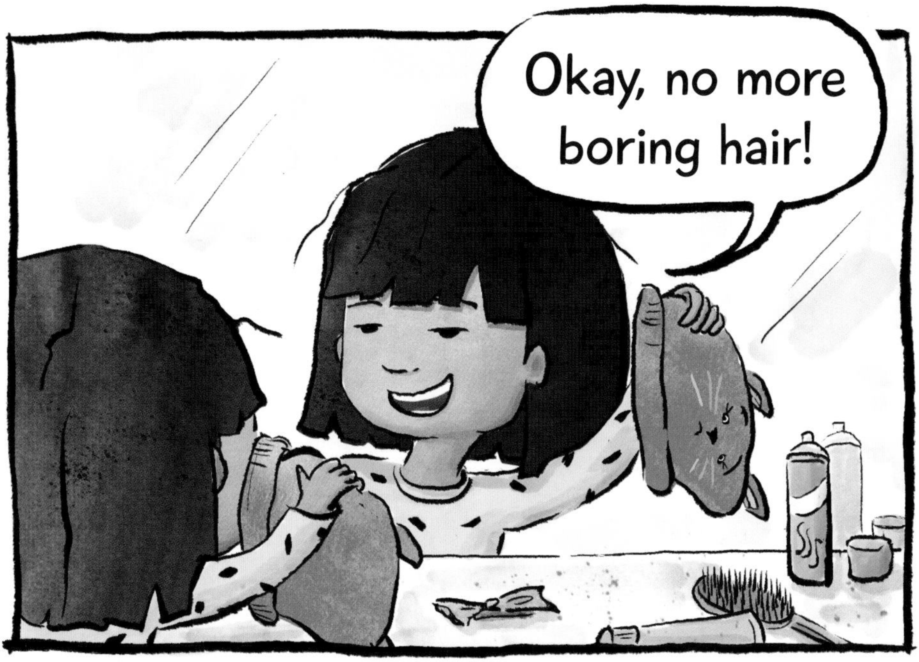
Okay, no more boring hair!

Then she brushes...

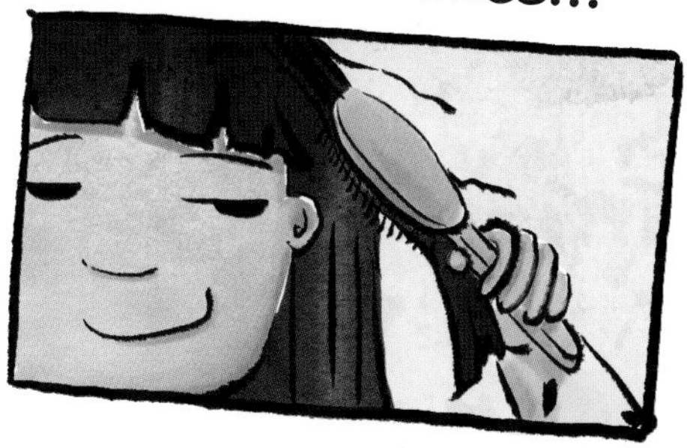

sprays...

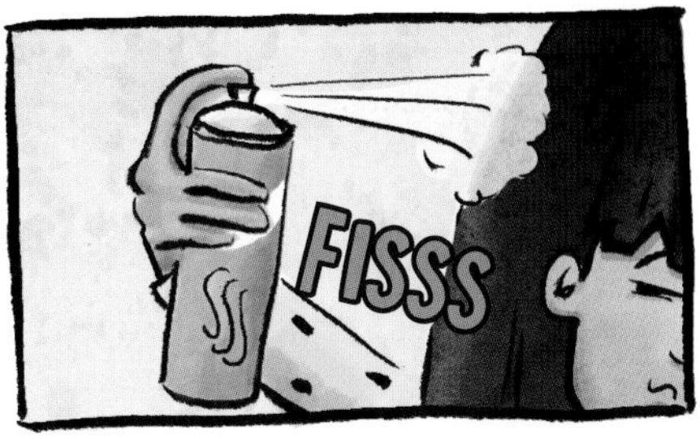
FISSS

wraps...

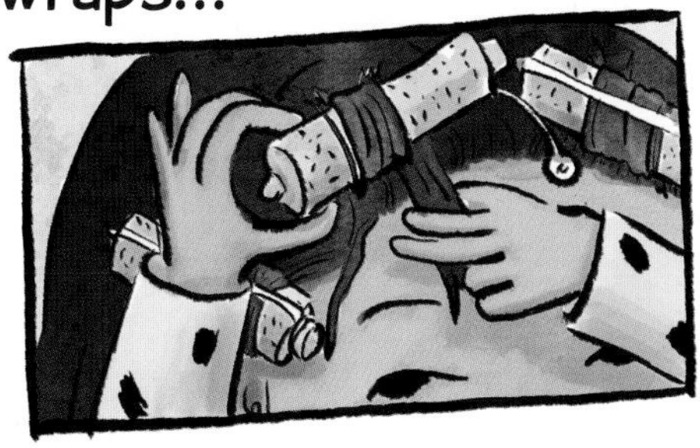

and squeezes gel...

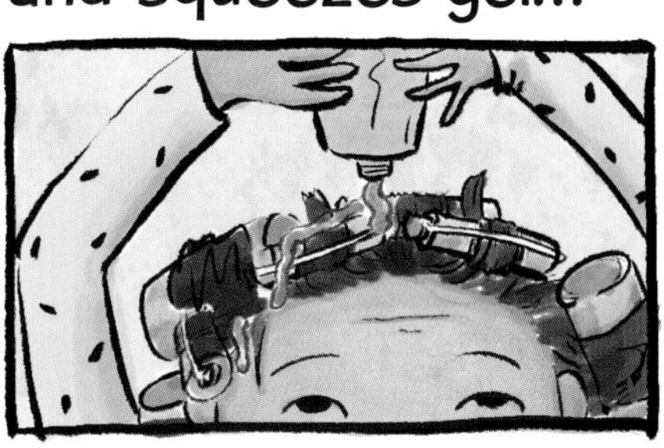

all over her head.

When Geraldine tries to remove the curlers, she yelps,

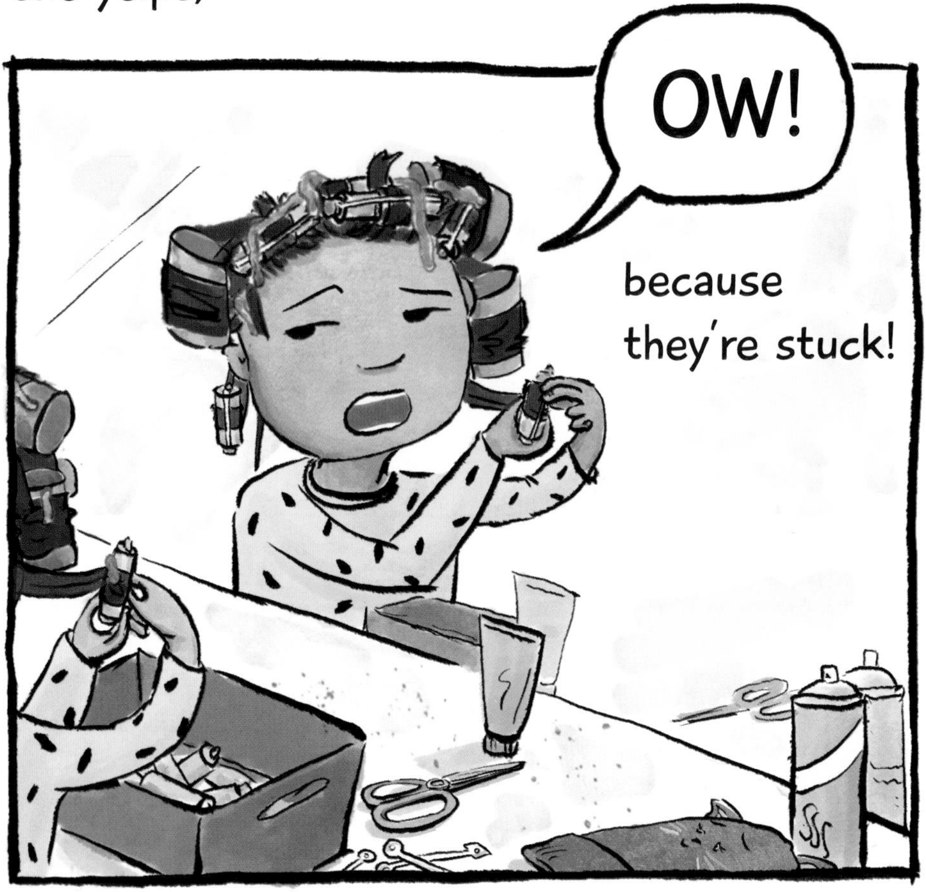
OW!
because they're stuck!

She mutters,

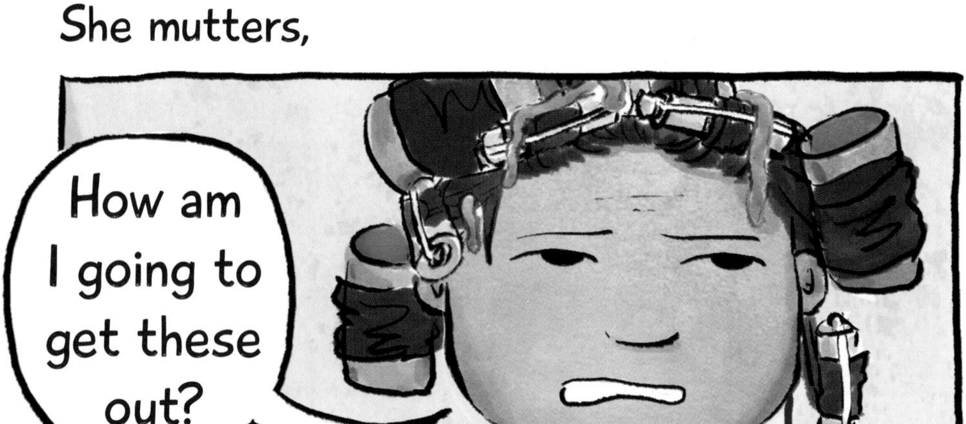
How am I going to get these out?

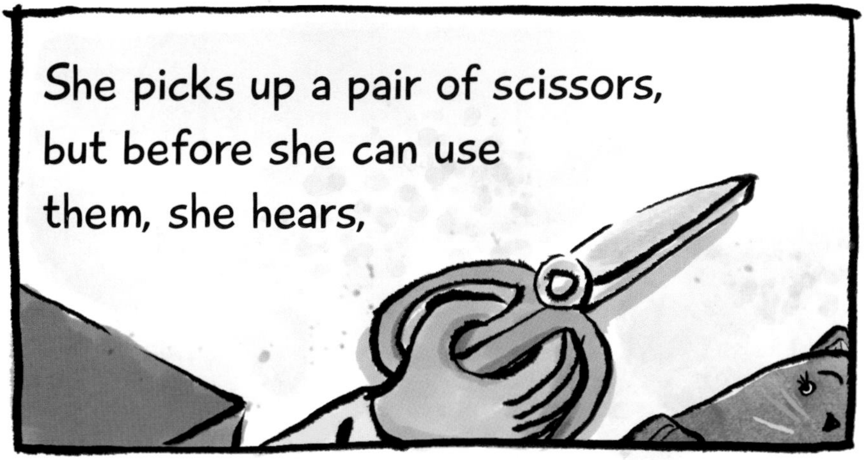
She picks up a pair of scissors, but before she can use them, she hears,

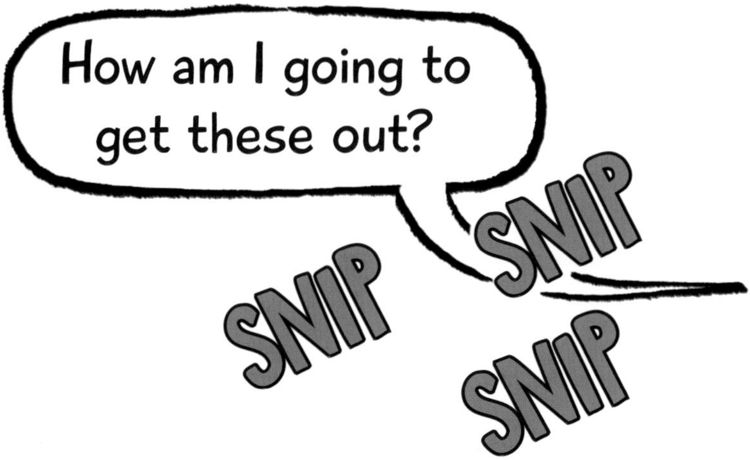
How am I going to get these out?
SNIP
SNIP
SNIP

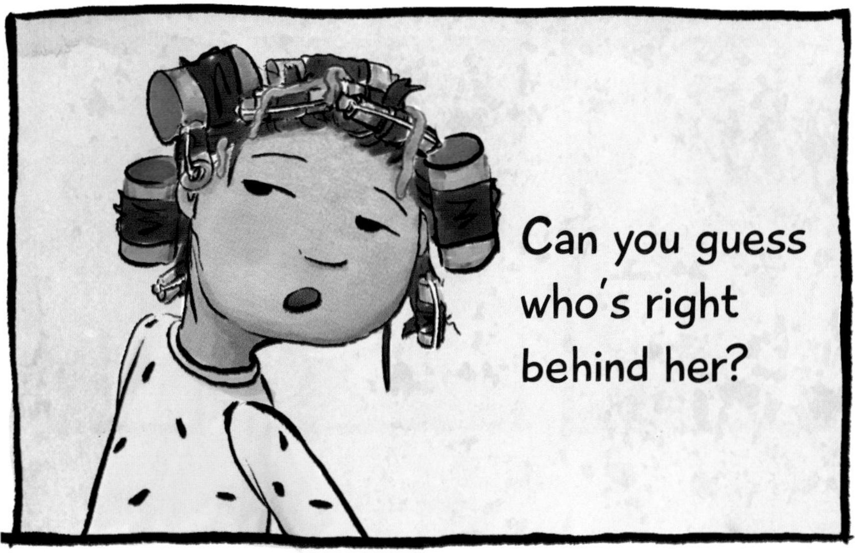
Can you guess who's right behind her?

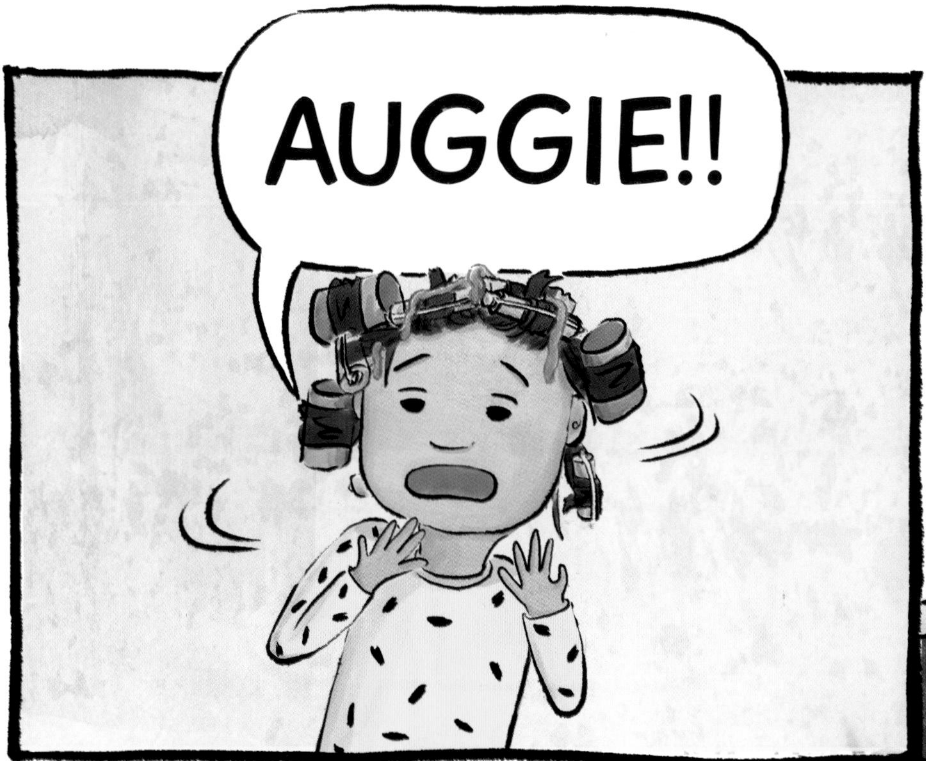
AUGGIE!!

Geraldine turns to find her brother and...

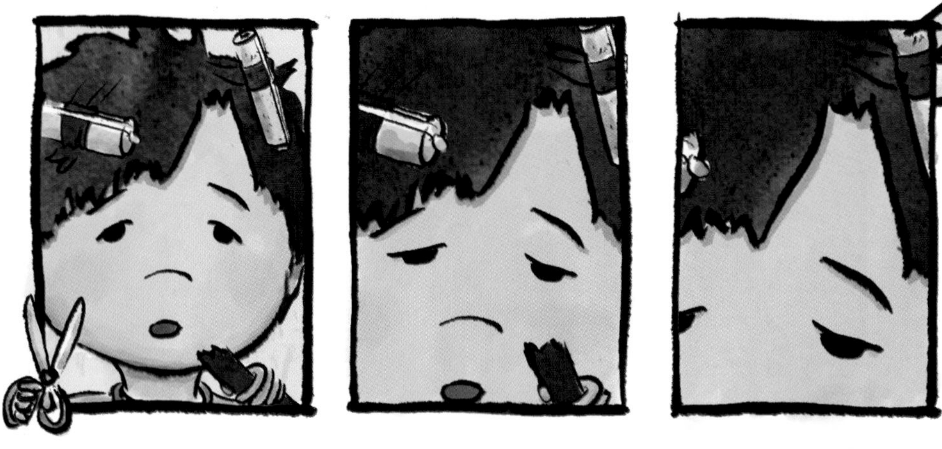

...a chunk of his hair missing!

When Auggie sees himself, he starts to cry,

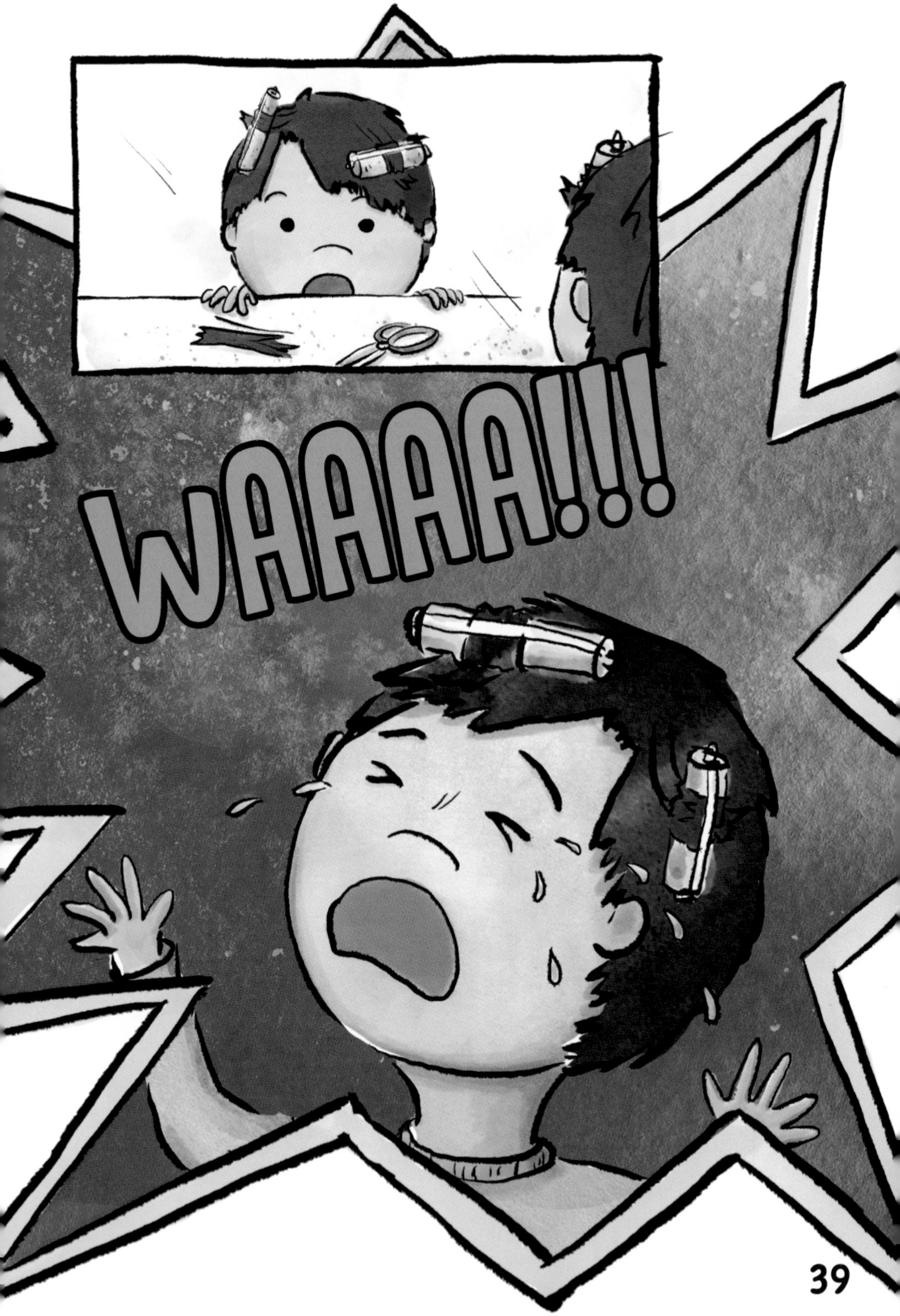
WAAAAA!!!!

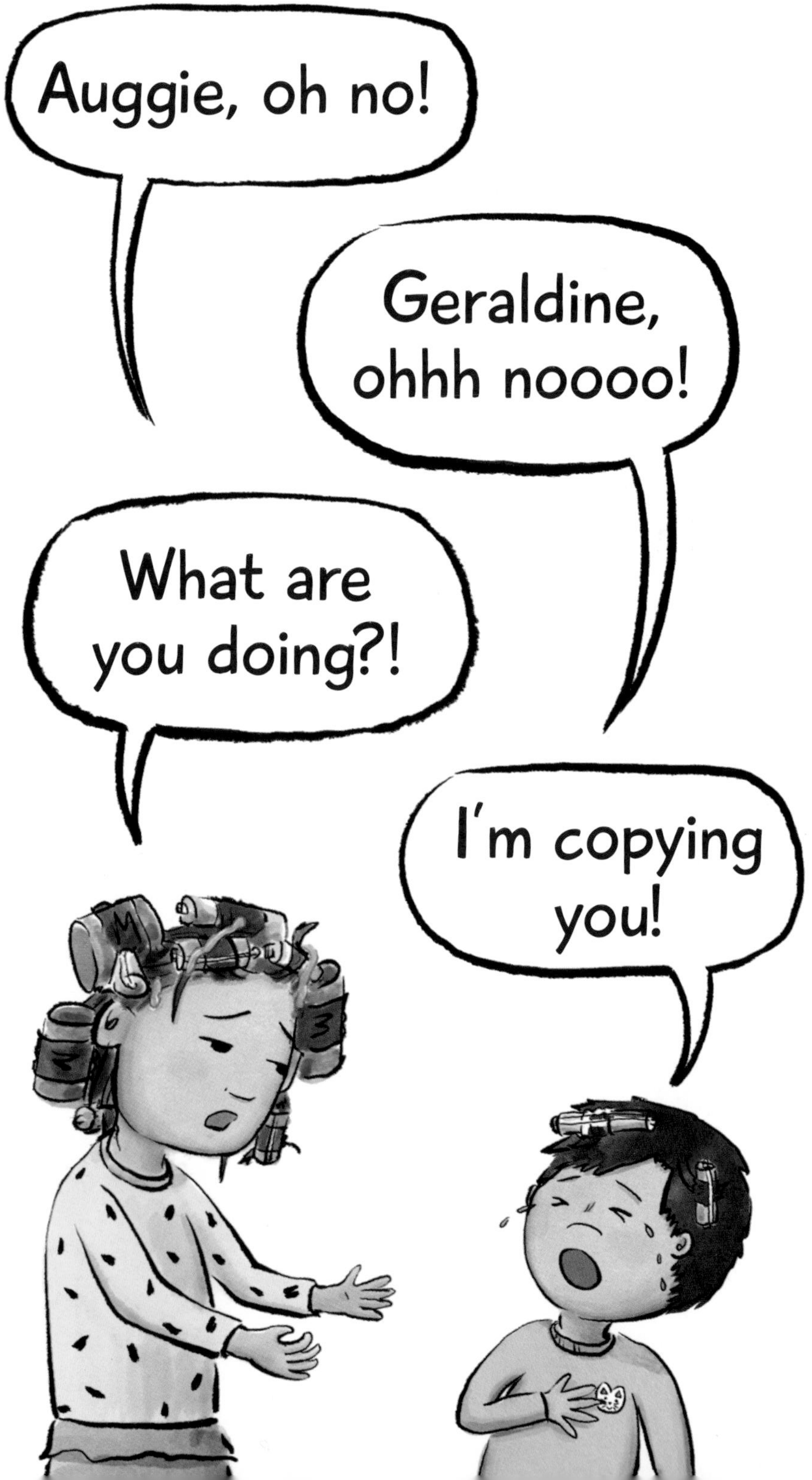
Auggie, oh no!
Geraldine, ohhh noooo!
What are you doing?!
I'm copying you!

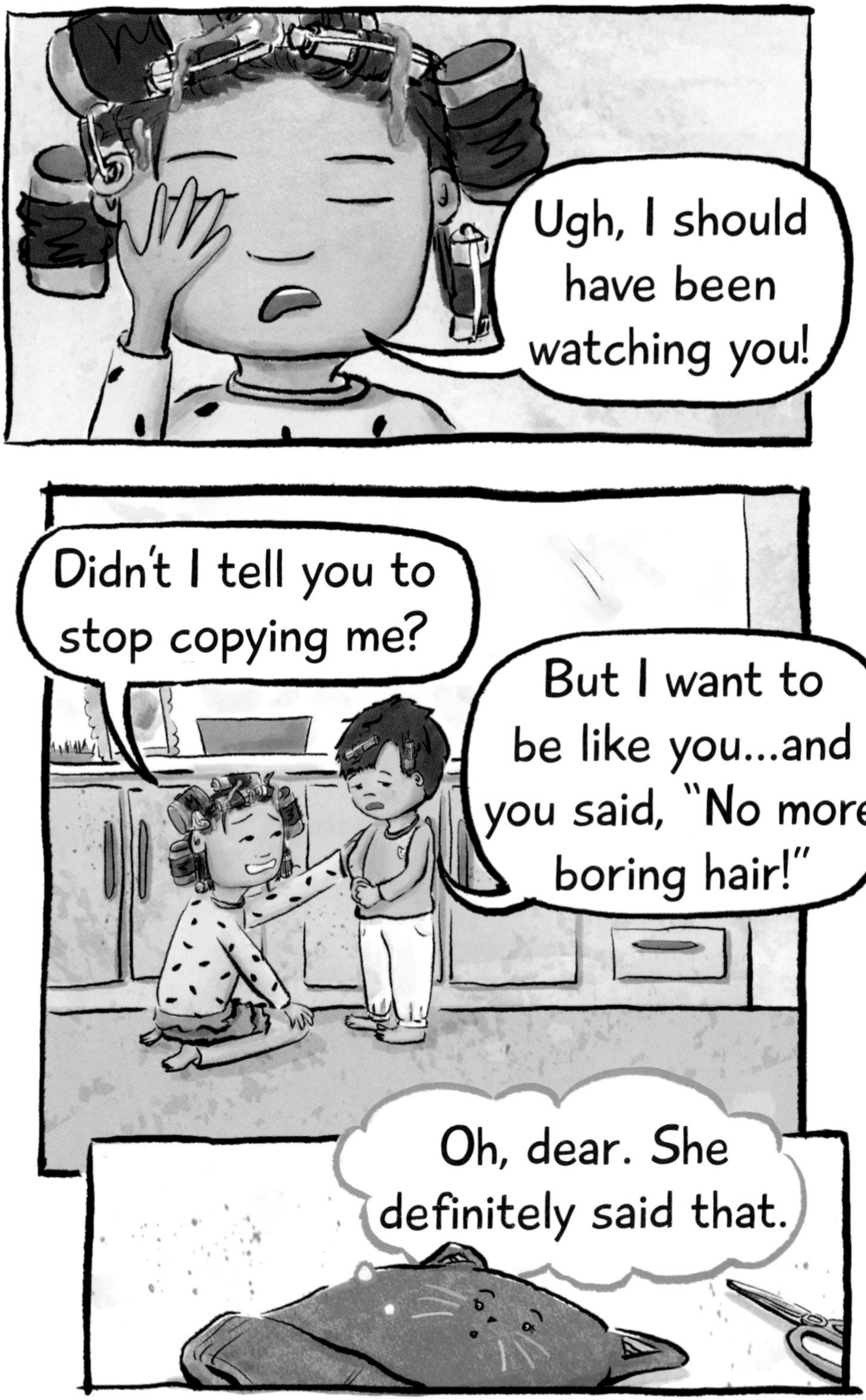
Ugh, I should have been watching you!
Didn't I tell you to stop copying me?
But I want to be like you...and you said, "No more boring hair!"
Oh, dear. She definitely said that.

Geraldine realizes Auggie wasn't the only copycat.

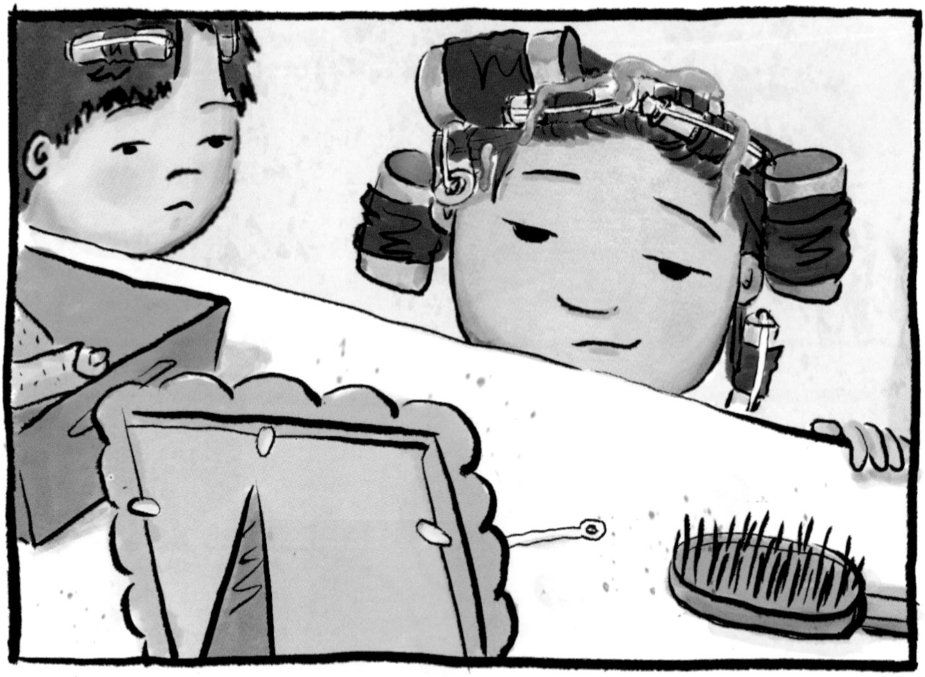

She was trying to copy Amah's hair for Picture Day.

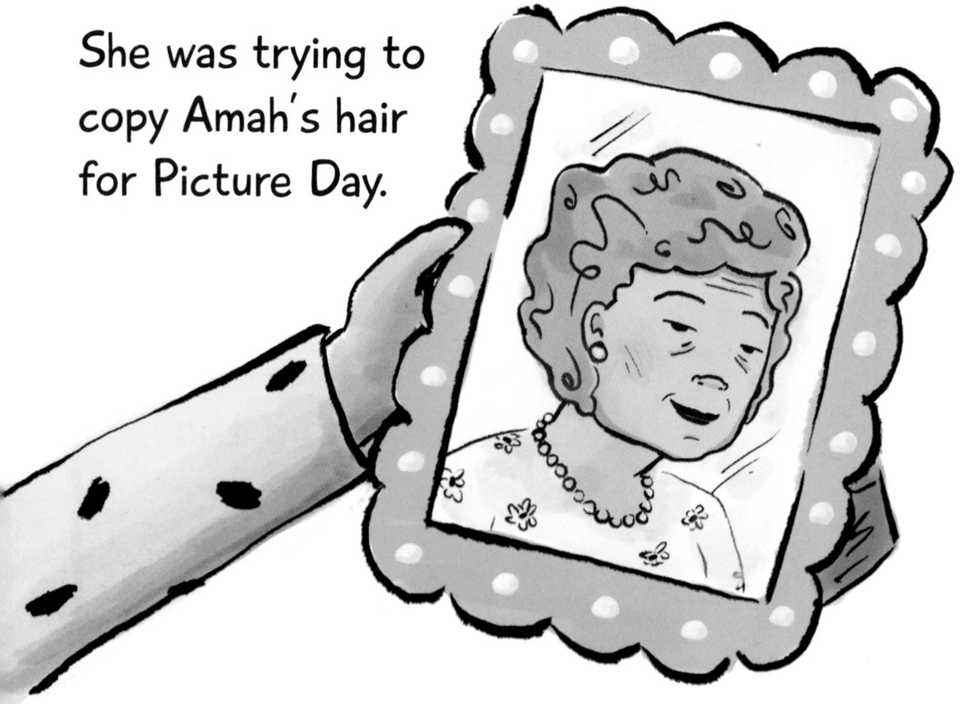

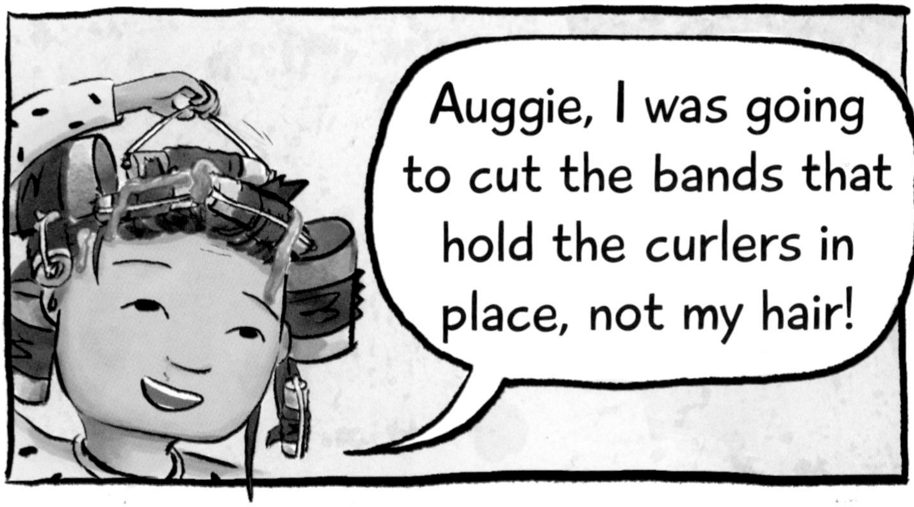
Auggie, I was going to cut the bands that hold the curlers in place, not my hair!

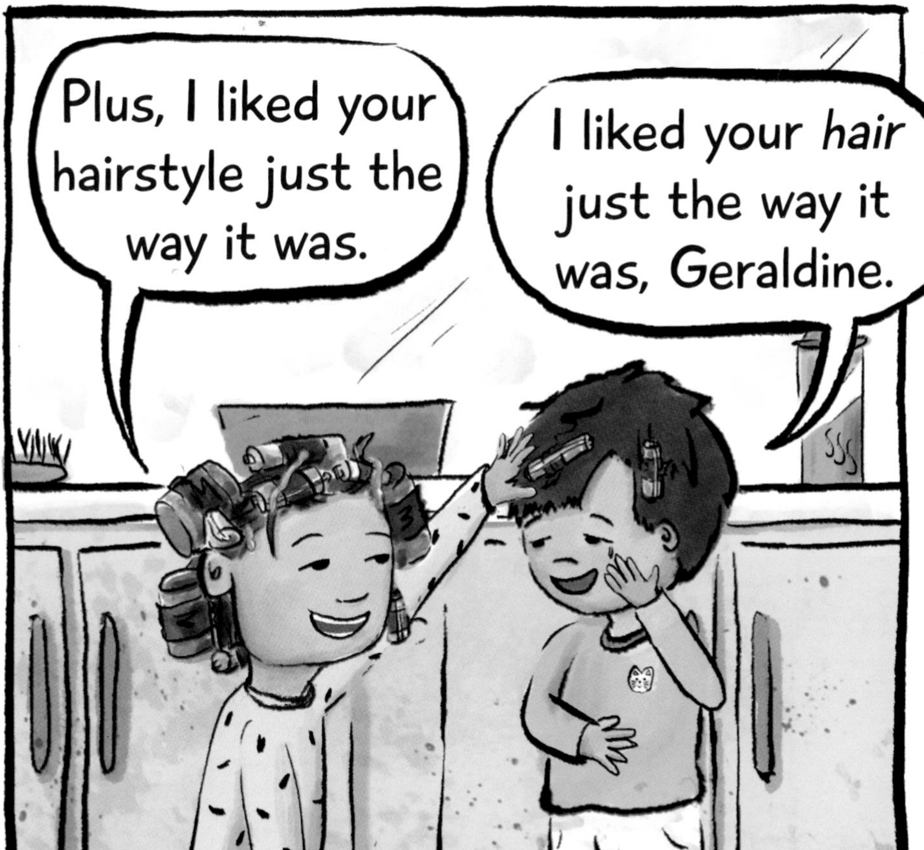
Plus, I liked your hairstyle just the way it was.
I liked your *hair* just the way it was, Geraldine.

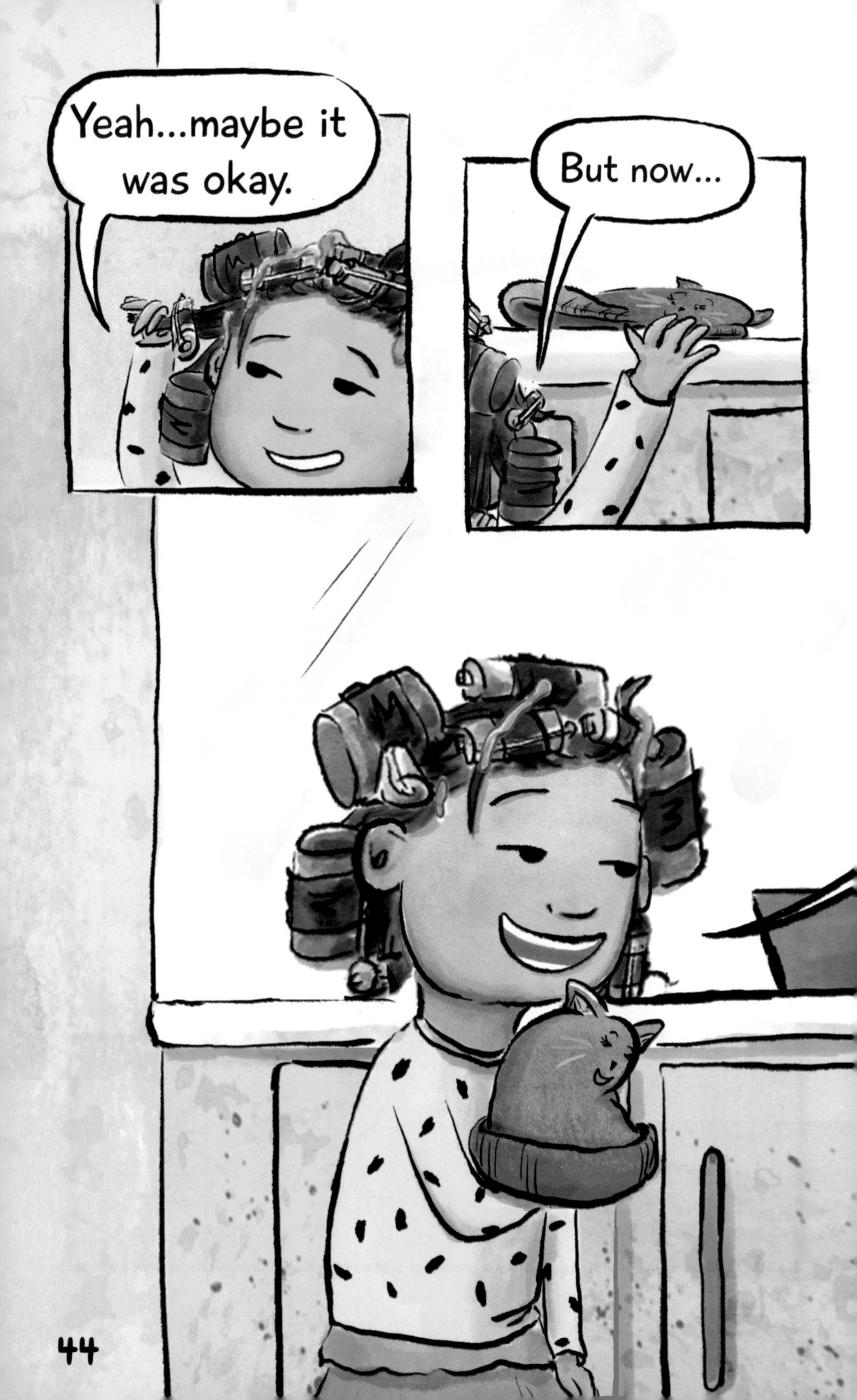
Yeah...maybe it was okay.
But now...

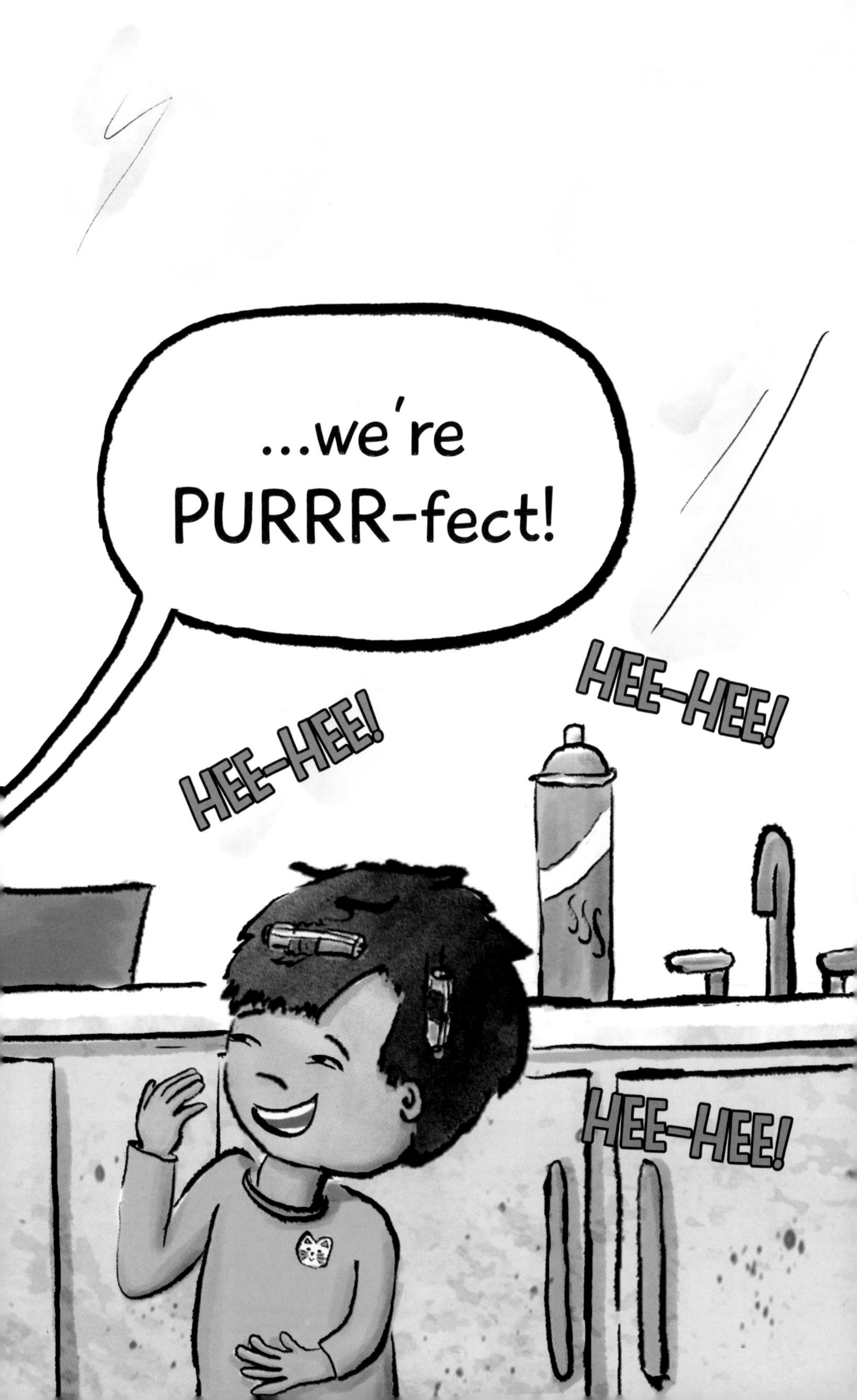
...we're
PURRR-fect!
HEE-HEE!
HEE-HEE!
HEE-HEE!

Soon, they can't stop laughing at how silly they look.

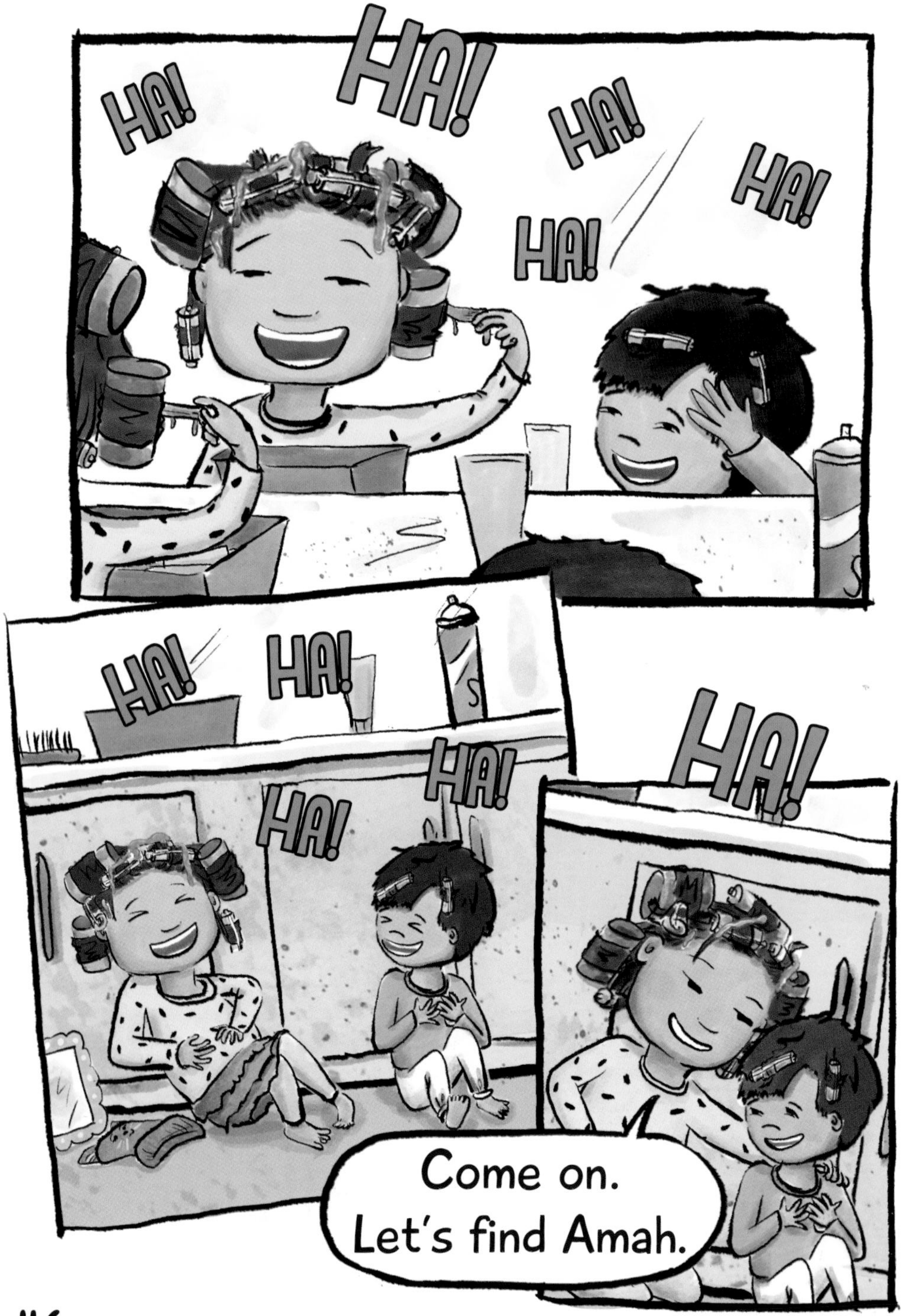
HA!
HA!
HA!
HA!
HA!
HA!
HA!
HA!
HA!
HA!
Come on.
Let's find Amah.

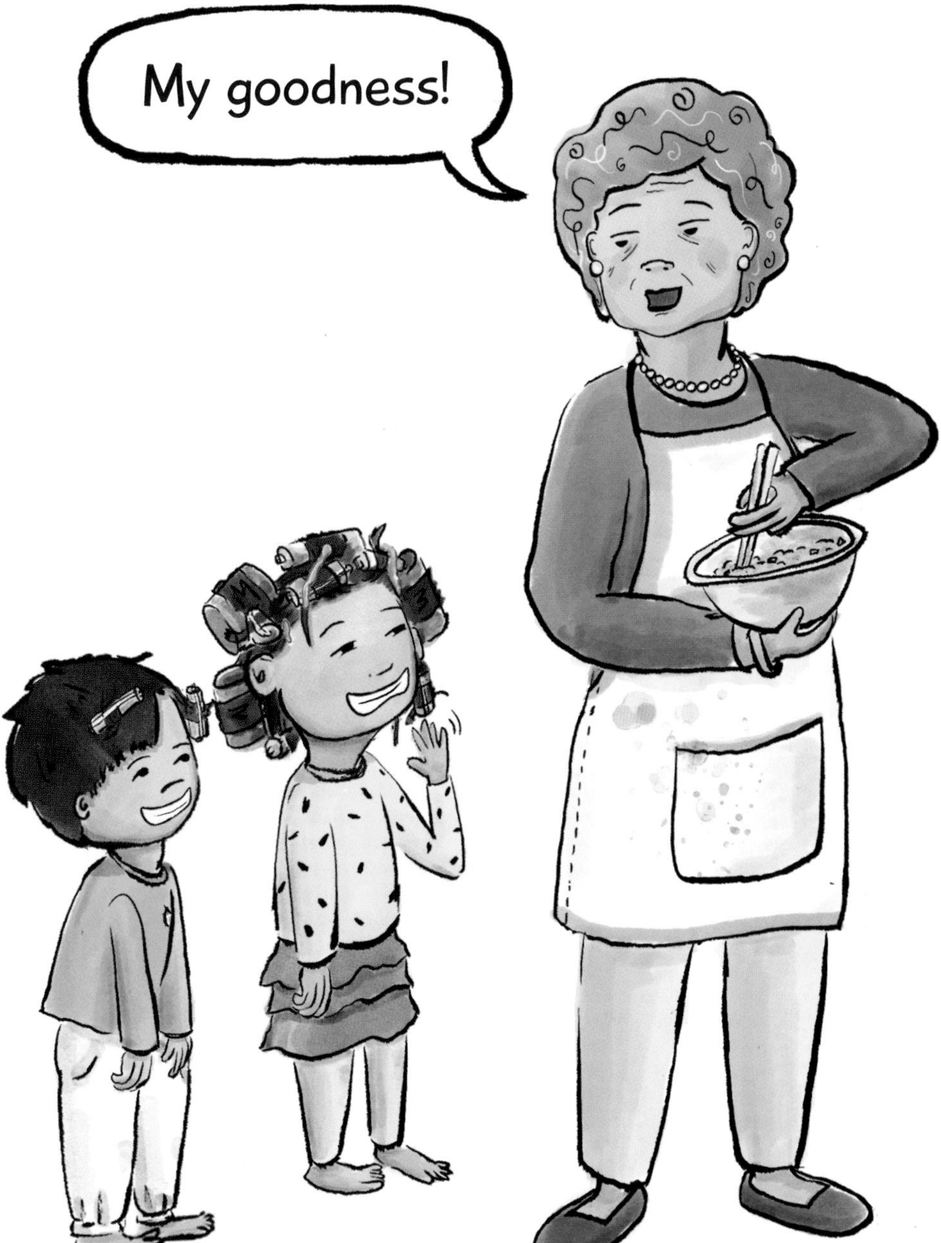
My goodness!

Chapter Four

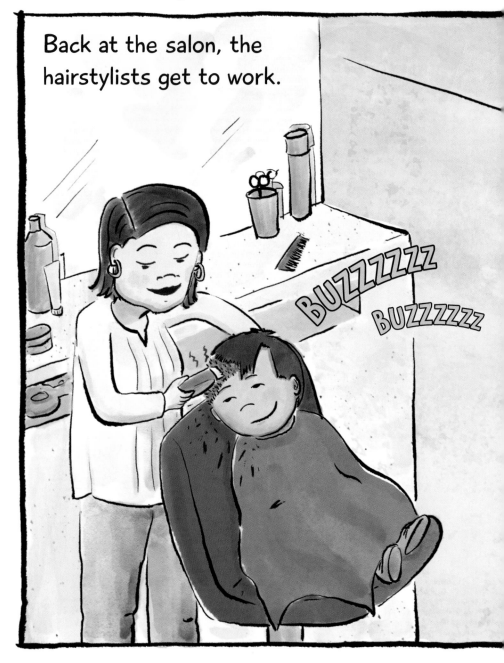

Back at the salon, the hairstylists get to work.

BUZZZZZZ
BUZZZZZZ

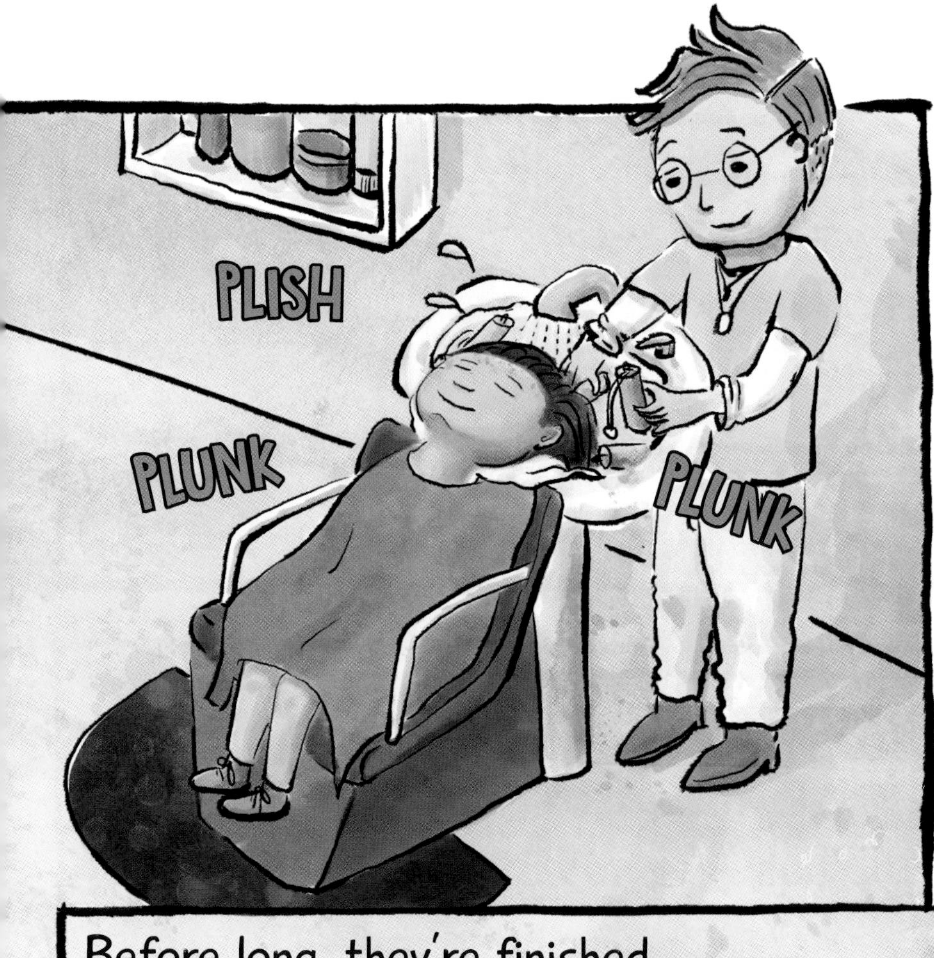
PLISH
PLUNK
PLUNK

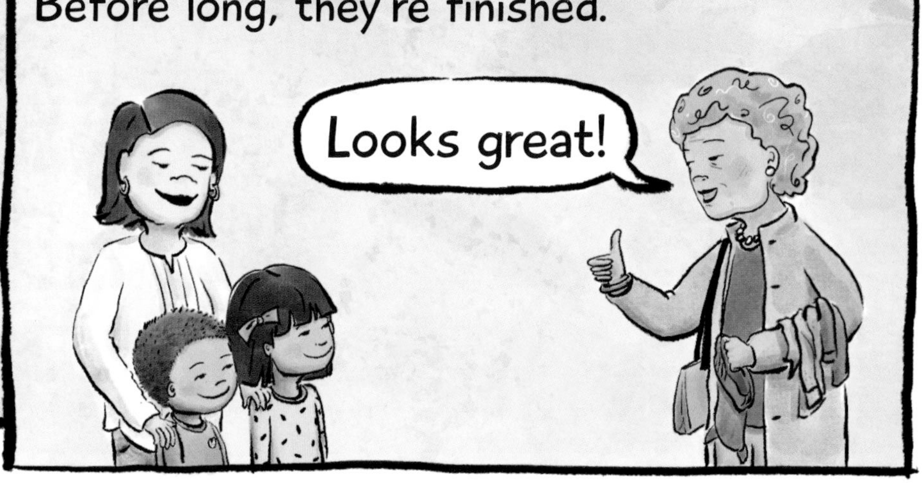
Before long, they're finished.
Looks great!

As they leave, Geraldine admits that she was trying to be like Amah.

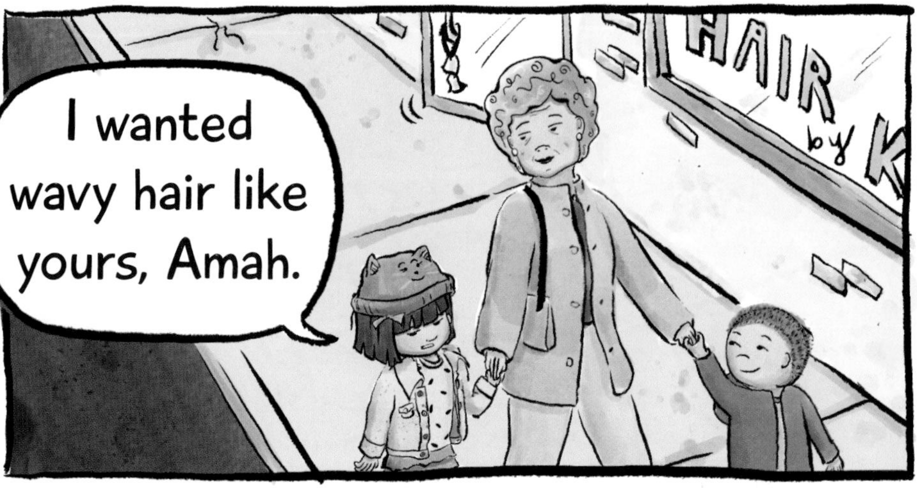
I wanted wavy hair like yours, Amah.
HAIR by K

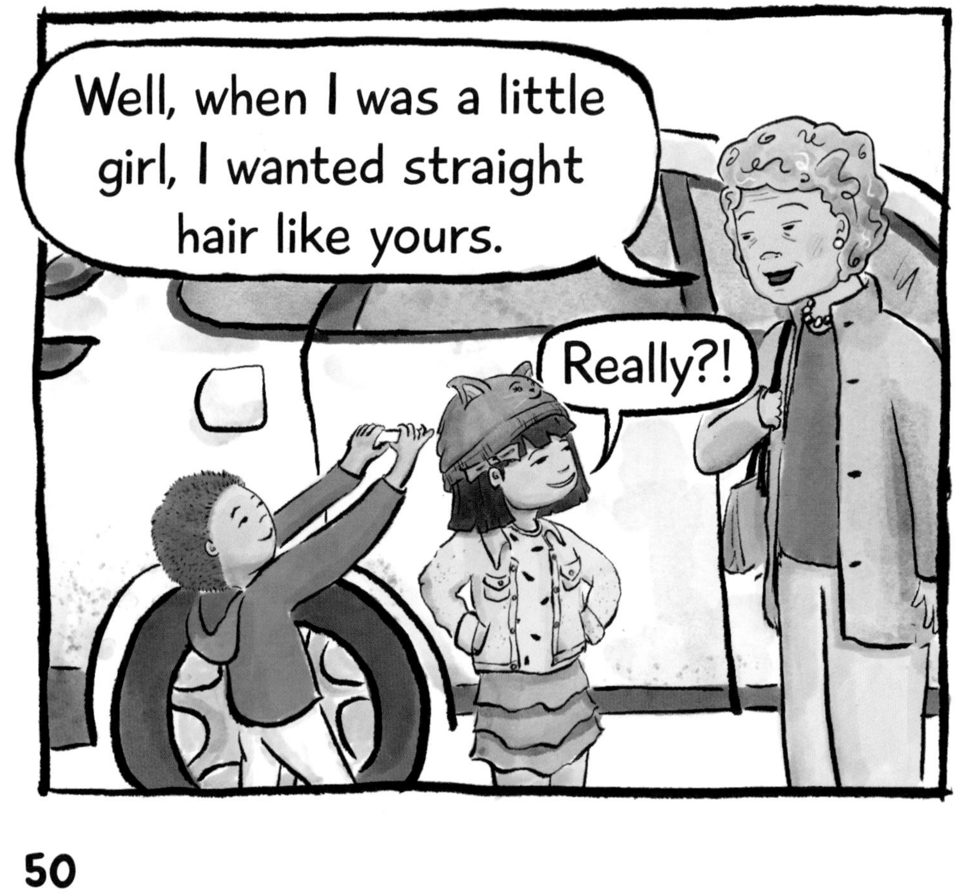
Well, when I was a little girl, I wanted straight hair like yours.
Really?!

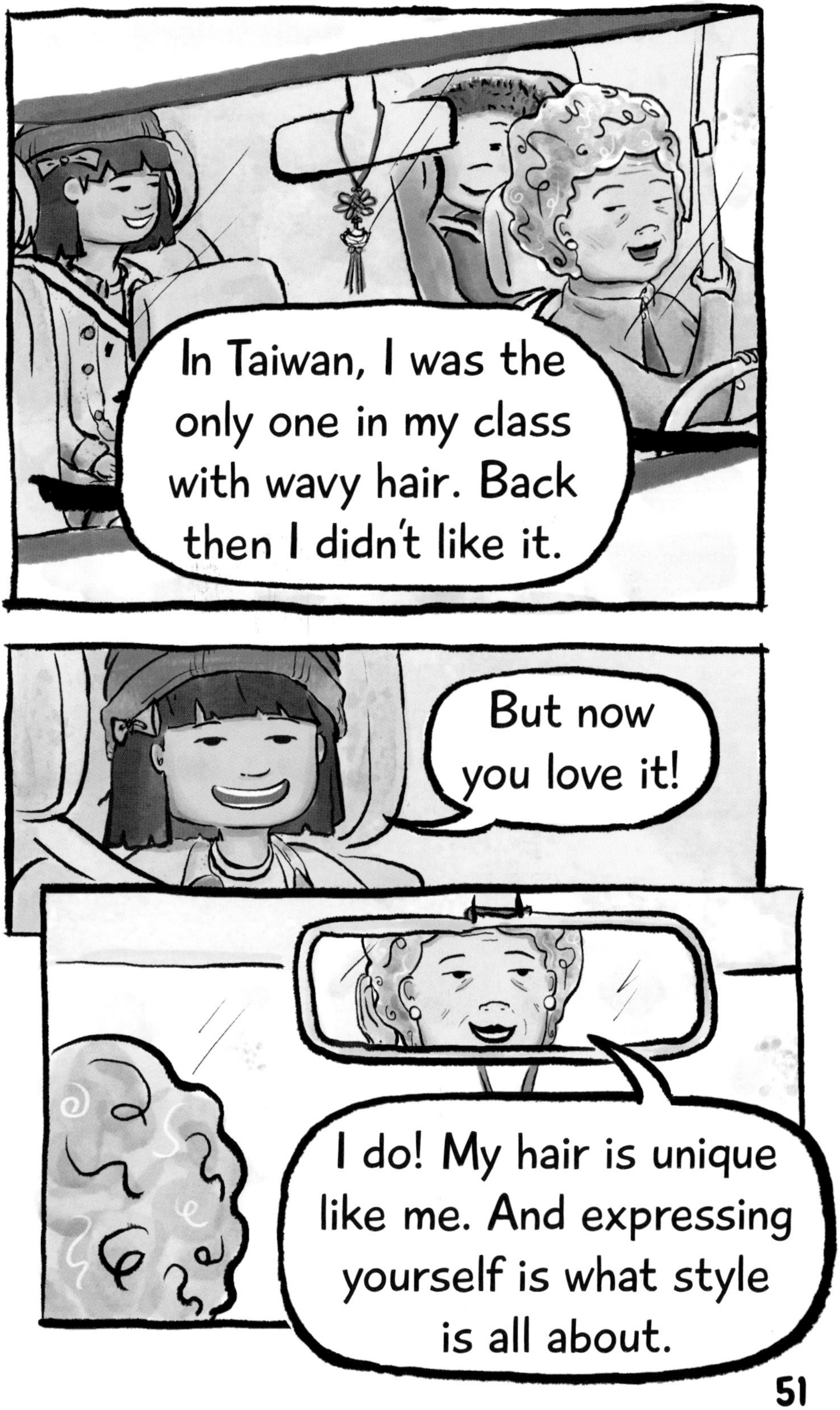
In Taiwan, I was the only one in my class with wavy hair. Back then I didn't like it.
But now you love it!
I do! My hair is unique like me. And expressing yourself is what style is all about.

Before she drives home, Amah tells them both,

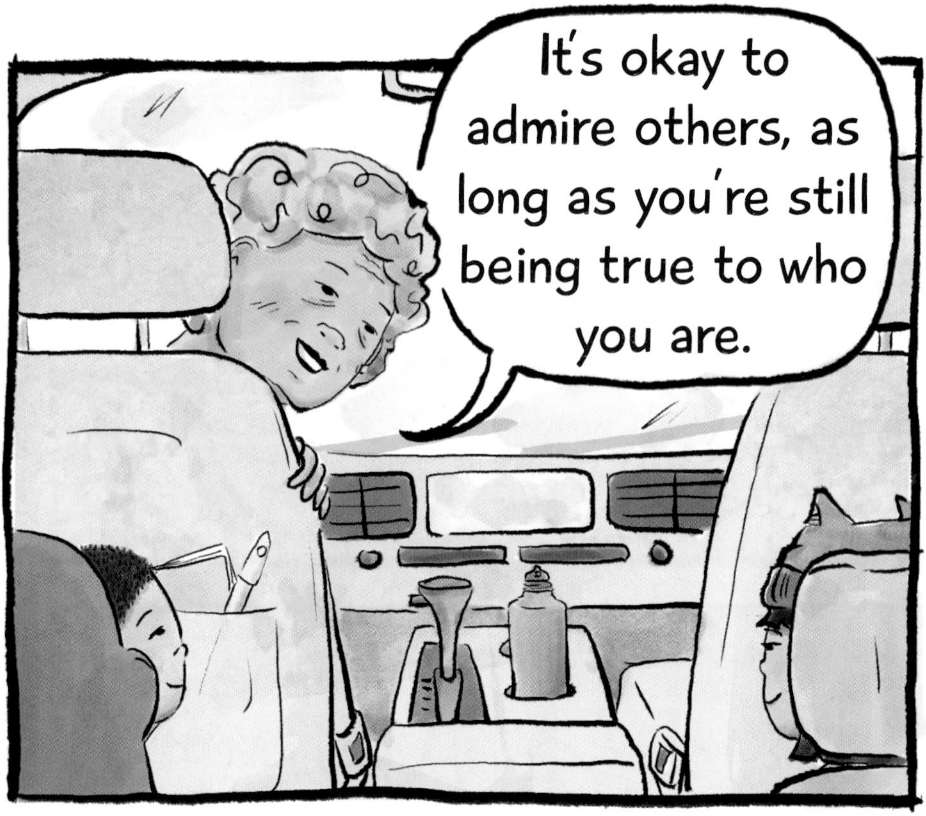
It's okay to admire others, as long as you're still being true to who you are.

Geraldine thinks about this and says to Auggie,

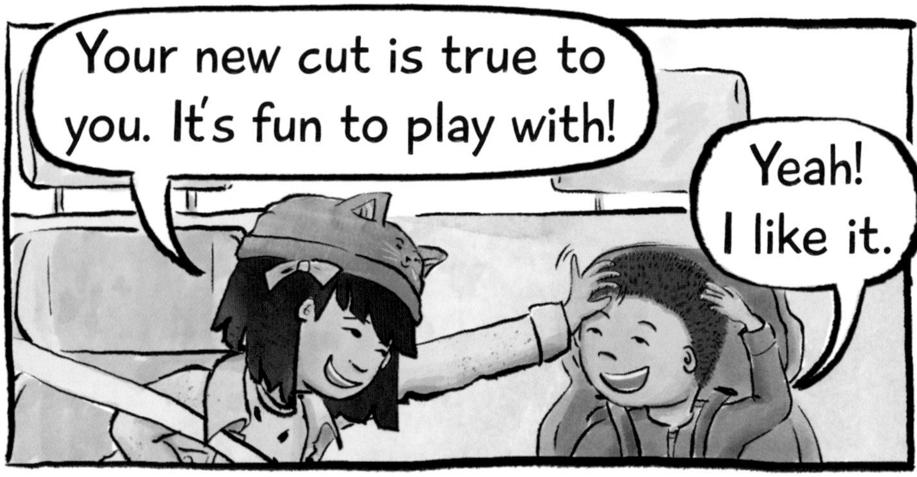
Your new cut is true to you. It's fun to play with!
Yeah! I like it.

But Auggie's short hair makes him feel cold.

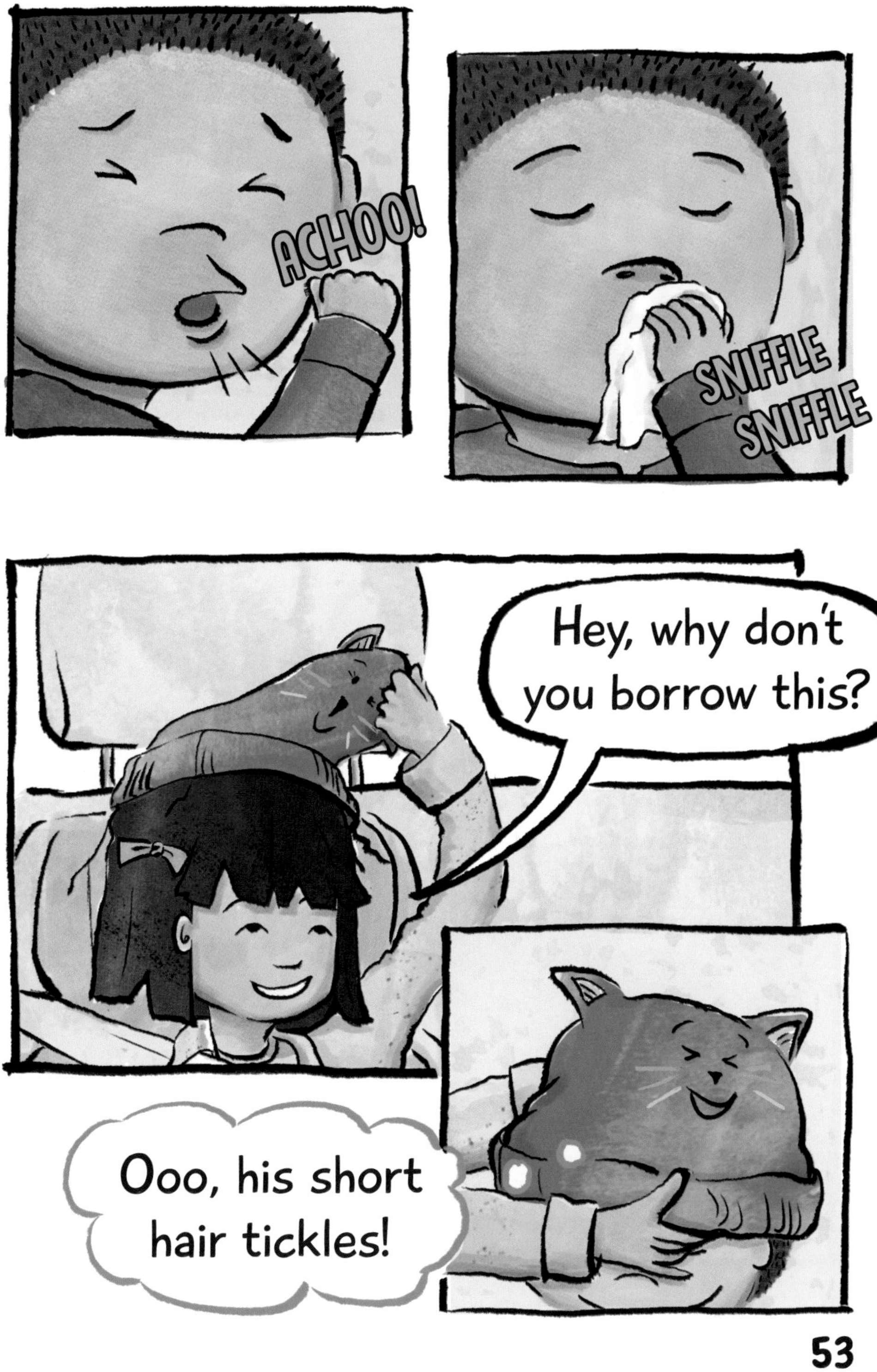
ACHOO!
SNIFFLE
SNIFFLE
Hey, why don't you borrow this?
Ooo, his short hair tickles!

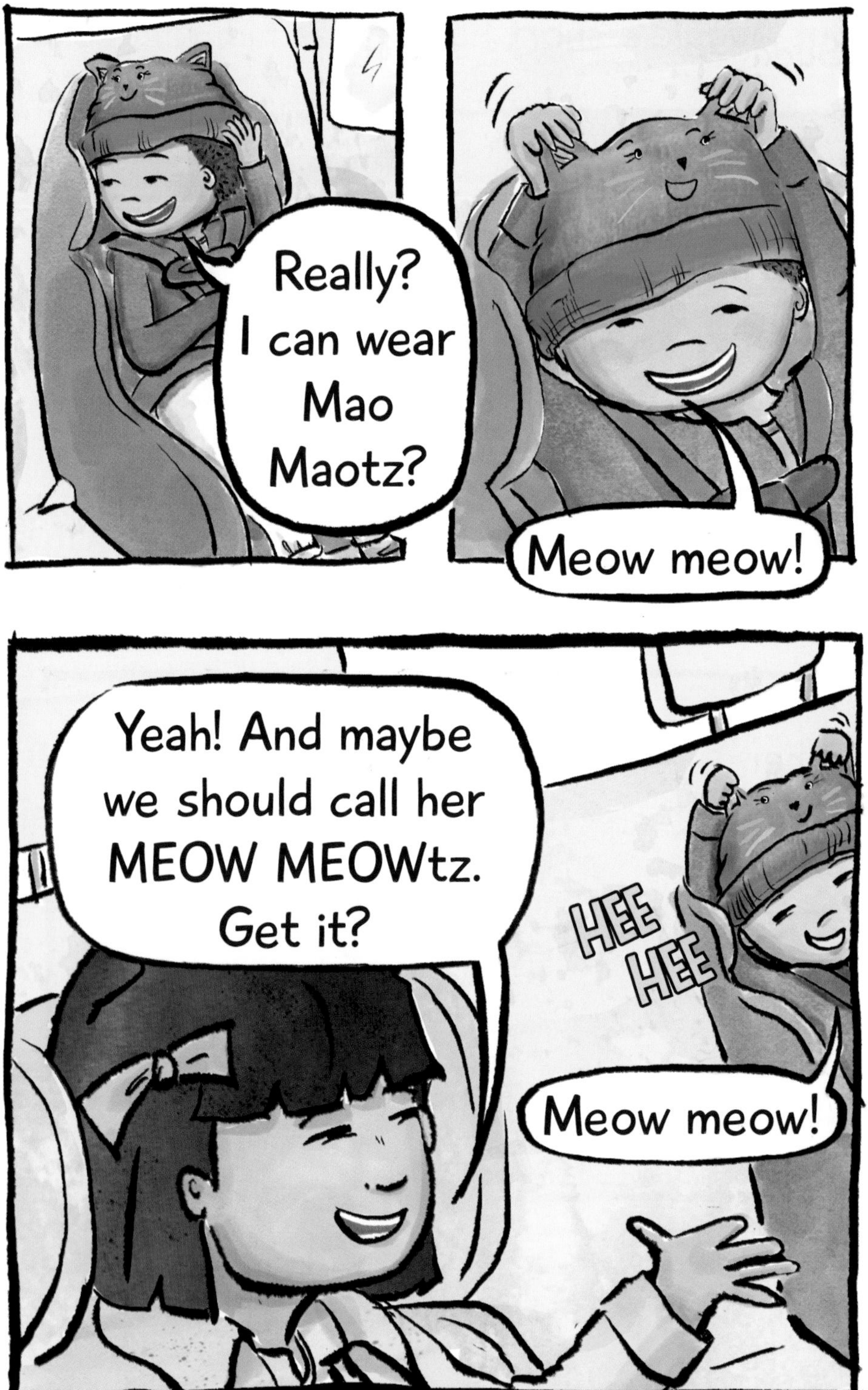
Really? I can wear Mao Maotz?
Meow meow!
Yeah! And maybe we should call her MEOW MEOWtz. Get it?
HEE HEE
Meow meow!

Suddenly, Geraldine shouts,

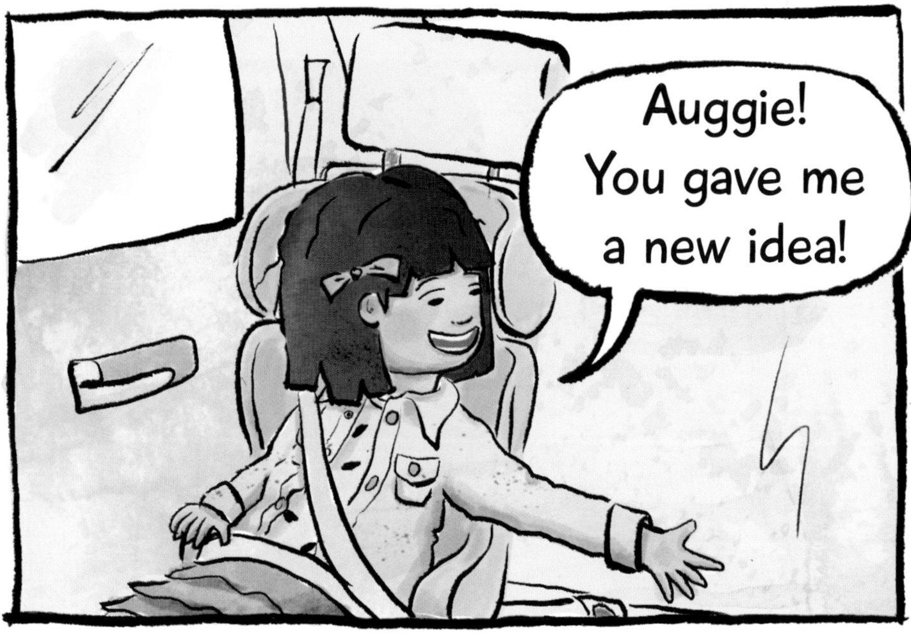
Auggie!
You gave me
a new idea!

When she gets home
she gathers supplies
for her new project!

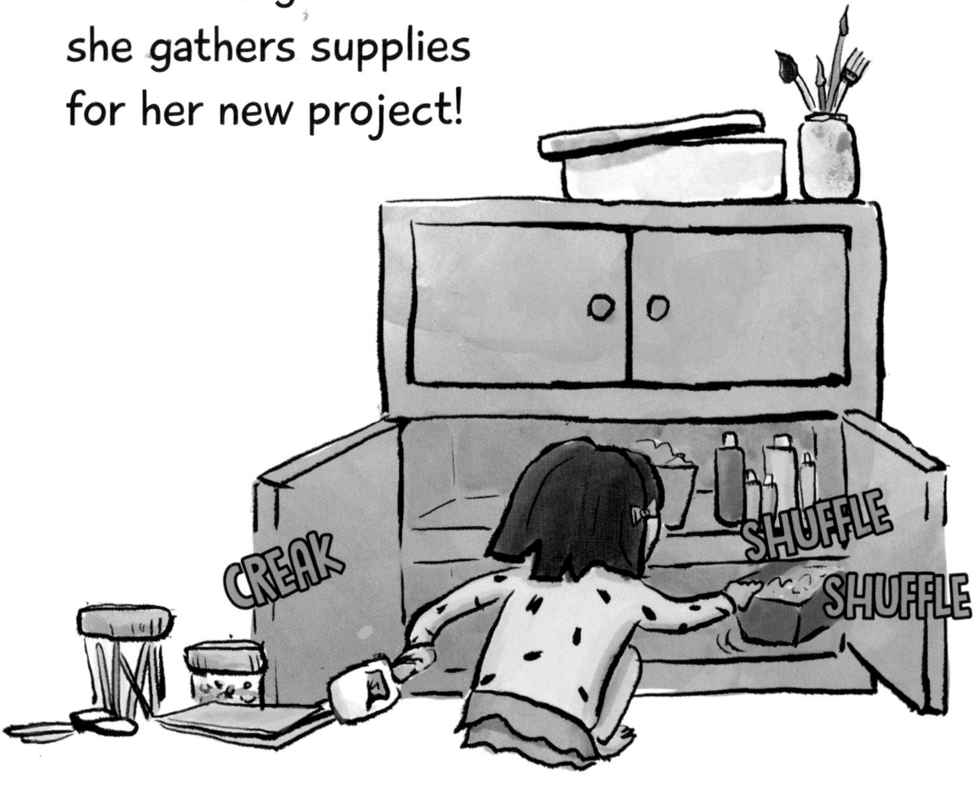
CREAK
SHUFFLE
SHUFFLE

In the morning Geraldine lets Auggie borrow her hat again.

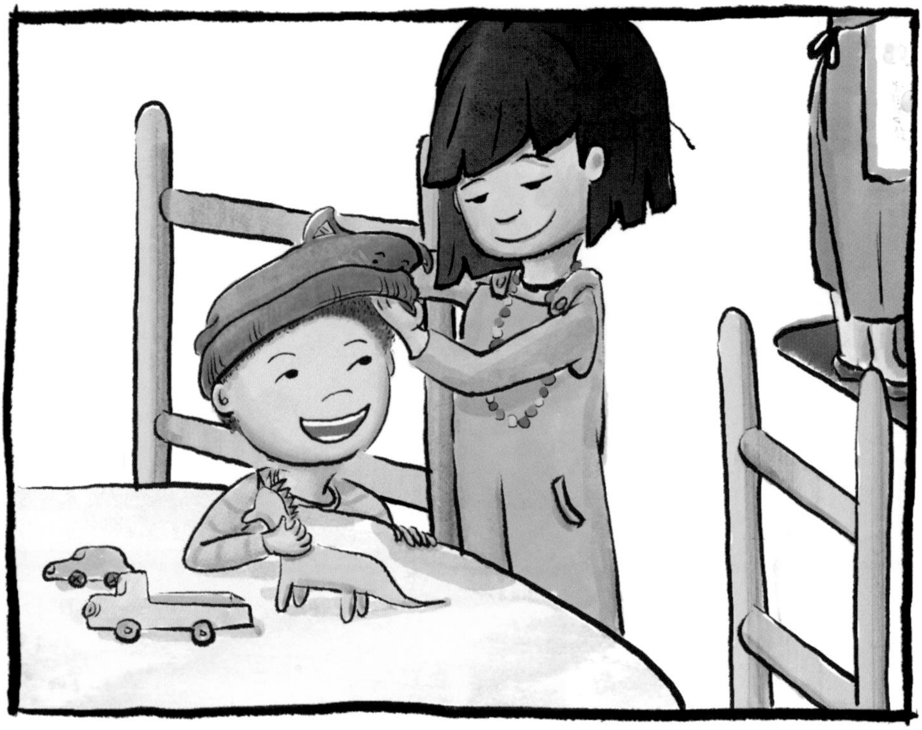

For her own head she has a brand-new, homemade...

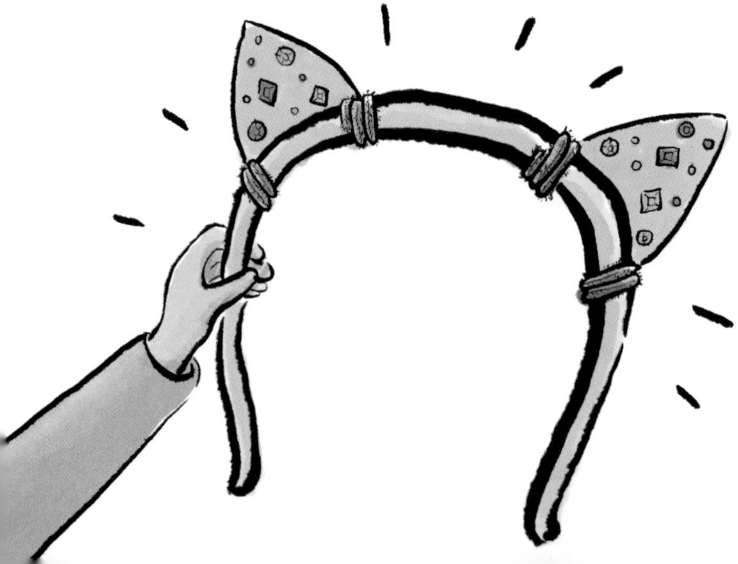

...cat headband!

Geraldine explains,

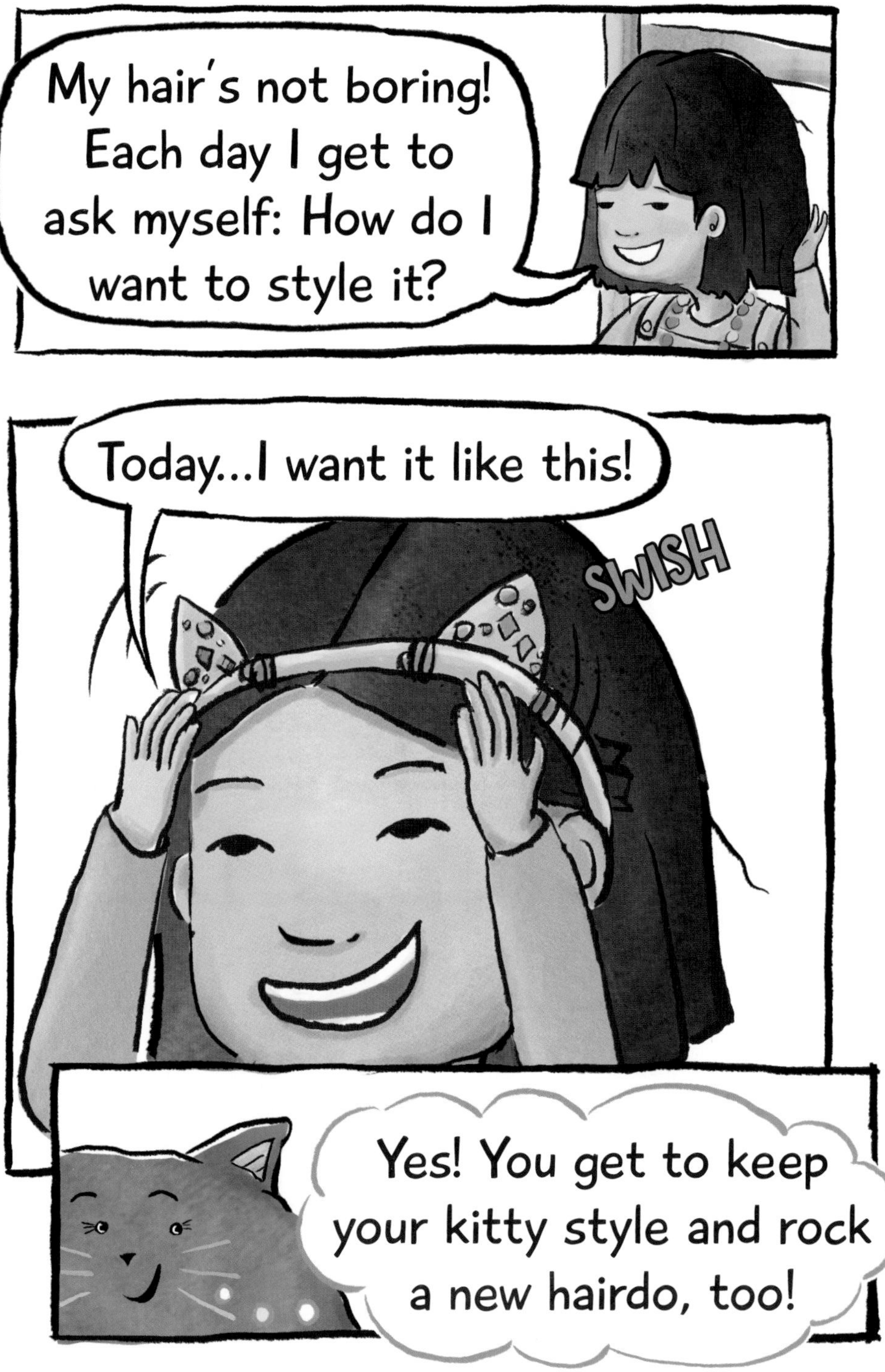
My hair's not boring! Each day I get to ask myself: How do I want to style it?
Today...I want it like this!
SWISH
Yes! You get to keep your kitty style and rock a new hairdo, too!

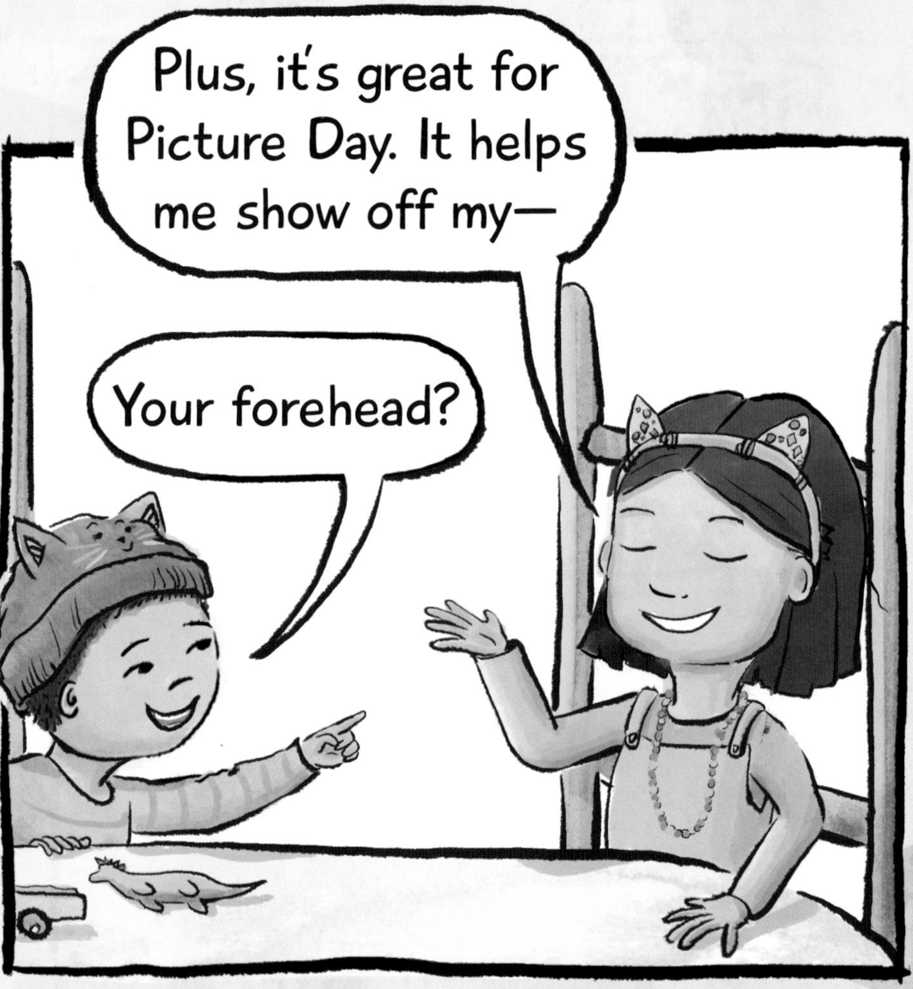
Plus, it's great for Picture Day. It helps me show off my—
Your forehead?

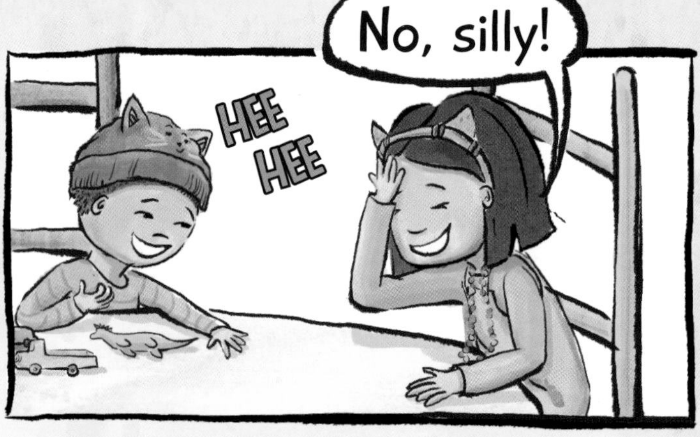
No, silly!
HEE HEE

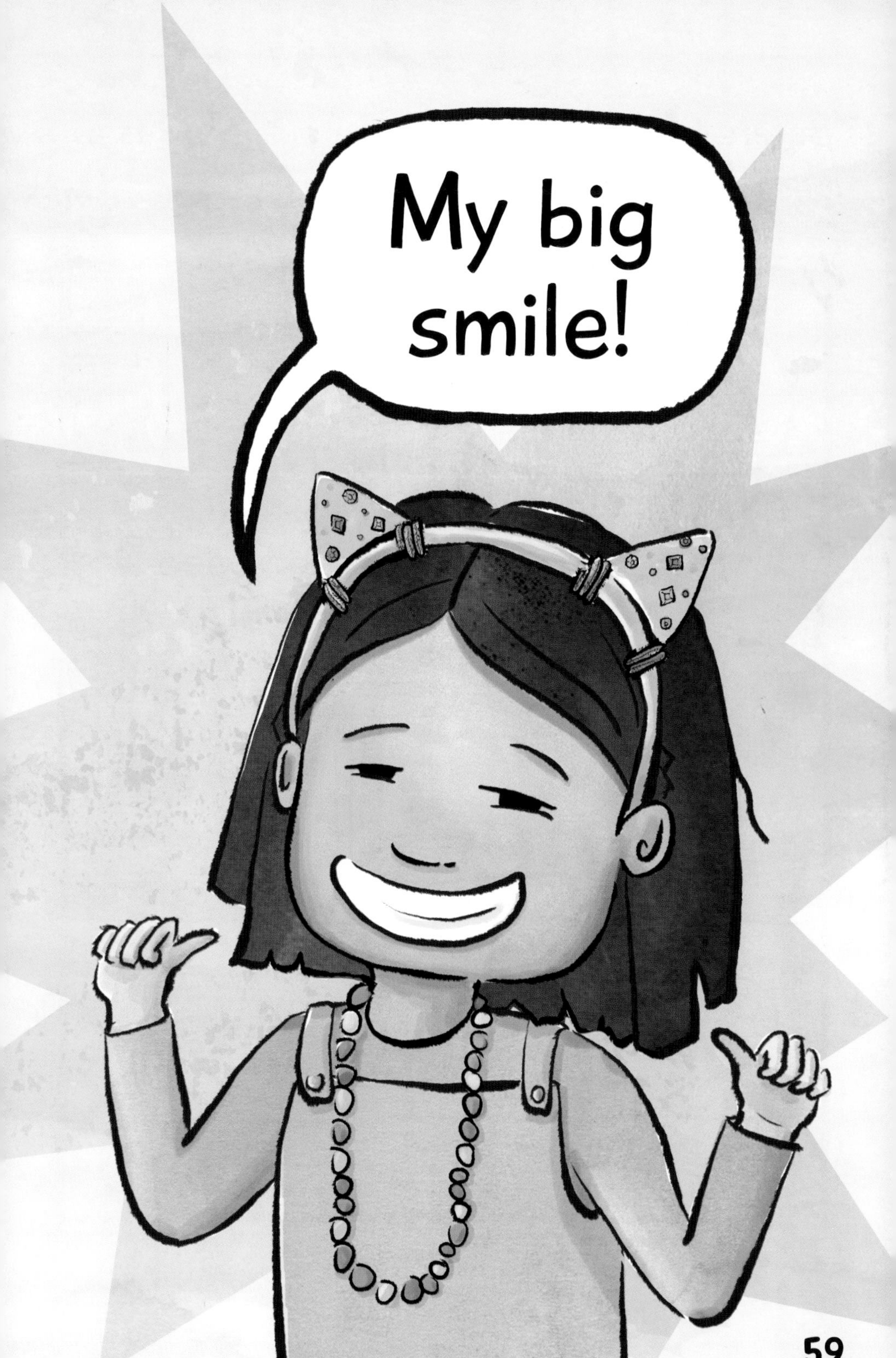
My big smile!

Before leaving for school, Geraldine takes a peek in the mirror and says,

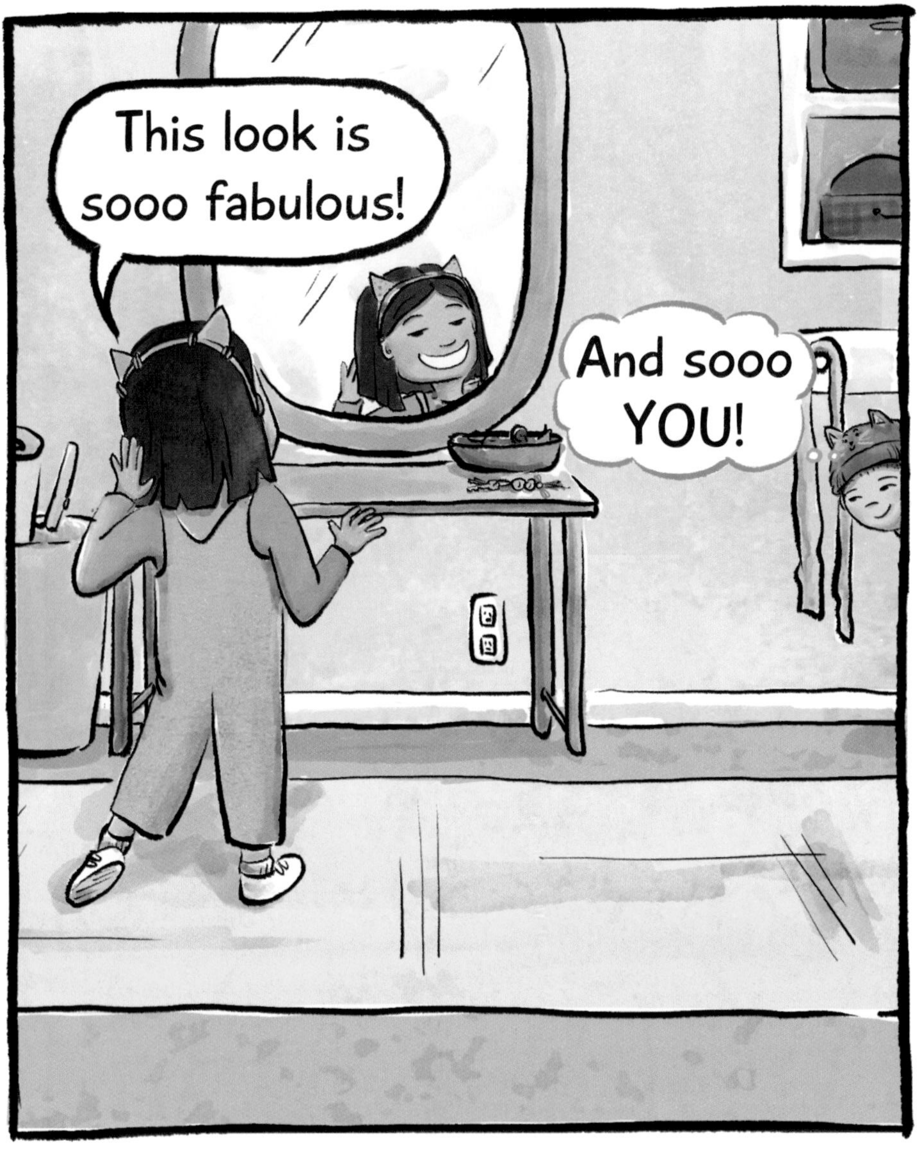
This look is sooo fabulous!
And sooo YOU!

The End

A MESSAGE FROM MAO MAOTZ

People throughout the world are born with all different kinds of hair. It's great! In fact, sometimes people within the same family have different hair textures, like Geraldine and Amah do. Their hair is not the only thing that is different for Geraldine and Amah: When Amah was a child living in Taiwan in the 1960s, teachers wanted students to focus on studies instead of hairstyles. So, the school's rule was that every girl had to have the same short haircut. Because her classmates all had straight hair, Amah's wavy hair really stood out! Each year she would have to convince her teachers that her waves were natural. After some time, Amah learned to love her unique hair, and now she thinks her waves look great.

Throughout history, many hair trends have come and gone, but one thing has always stayed the same—people use their hair to express themselves! Similar to how your frowns and smiles can help others understand your feelings, what you do with your hair and what you wear on your head can be a way to share part of yourself. Your hair is yours, no matter what the color, how straight or curly, how long or short, and whether you have a lot of it or very little. So take care of it and have fun! And remember, expressing yourself is what style is all about!

What do you love about *your* hair?

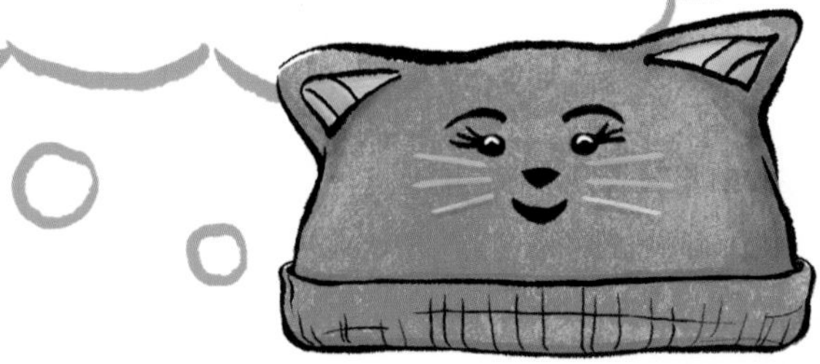

HOW TO MAKE A SELF-PORTRAIT COLLAGE

Another fun way people express themselves is through self-portraits. A self-portrait is art you make that is of yourself. There are many kinds of self-portraits, and this activity uses a mix of materials glued to paper to create a picture of your face. Art made from combining different materials is called a collage (said like this: kuh-LAHJ).

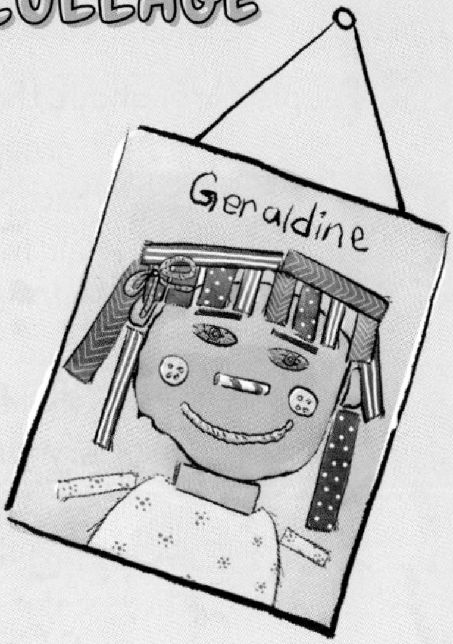
Geraldine

Step 1. Ask an adult to help you gather supplies:

- scissors
- glue
- mirror
- 2 pieces of paper: 1 for your background and 1 for notes
- collage materials of all different textures and colors like paper, cardboard, scraps of fabric, felt, yarn, ribbon, buttons, beads, gems, materials from the recycling bin, and everyday objects like small plastic spoons and straws. Anything that you are okay gluing down will do! You may even think of other materials to use when you're making your collage.

Step 2. Look in the mirror. What do you notice about your face? Ask a grown-up to help you write down what you see on a piece of paper.

Step 3. Use your notes from step 2 and your materials to make a self-portrait! First, use the other piece of blank paper as the background of your self-portrait. Then, start with your head. What

material reminds you of this part of you? Cut out or arrange the shape you need and place it on your background paper.
For example, did you notice your head is round? If so, pick a material that has a color and texture that reminds you of your head and cut out a circle.

Step 4. Which part of your head or face would you like to add next? Your hair? Eyes? Nose? Keep going until you feel you've captured all the parts that make you you!

Tip: You can tell how people might be feeling by the way their mouths look. When you create your mouth for your collage, you can cut or arrange a shape to show how you are feeling—like a big, curved smile if you're feeling happy, or straight lips if you're feeling serious.

Step 5. Glue down all the materials you've arranged for your collage.

Step 6. Sign your art by writing your name on the paper.

Step 7. Ta-da! You have just made a self-portrait. Take a moment to admire your art!

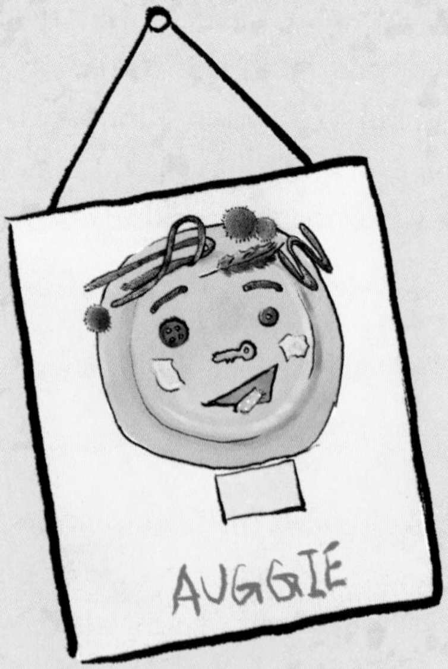
AUGGIE